CHARITY

ALSO BY KEATH FRASER

FICTION

Taking Cover
Foreign Affairs
Popular Anatomy
Telling My Love Lies
13 Ways of Listening to a Stranger
Damages: Selected Stories, 1982-2012

NON-FICTION

As for Me and My Body: A Memoir of Sinclair Ross
The Voice Gallery: Travels with a Glass Throat

ANTHOLOGIES

Bad Trips
Worst Journeys: The Picador Book of Travels

CHARITY

KEATH FRASER

A JOHN METCALF BOOK

BIBLIOASIS
WINDSOR, ONTARIO

FIRST EDITION

Library and Archives Canada Cataloguing in Publication

Title: Charity / Keath Fraser.
Names: Fraser, Keath, author.
Identifiers: Canadiana (print) 20200372416 |
Canadiana (ebook) 20200372475 | ISBN 9781771963800
(softcover) | ISBN 9781771963817 (ebook)
Classification: LCC PS8561.R297 C53 2021 | DDC C813/.54—dc23

Edited by John Metcalf
Copyedited by Emily Donaldson
Cover and text designed by Gordon Robertson

 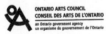

Published with the generous assistance of the Canada Council for the Arts, which last year invested $153 million to bring the arts to Canadians throughout the country, and the financial support of the Government of Canada. Biblioasis also acknowledges the support of the Ontario Arts Council (OAC), an agency of the Government of Ontario, which last year funded 1,709 individual artists and 1,078 organizations in 204 communities across Ontario, for a total of $52.1 million, and the contribution of the Government of Ontario through the Ontario Book Publishing Tax Credit and Ontario Creates.

PRINTED AND BOUND IN CANADA

In memory of my sister
Teresa Taylor
who loved to read

and

Sarah McAlpine

He reckoneth without his Hostesse.
Love knoweth no lawes.

– Lyly

and for

Sally Elliott

Children are what the mothers are
No fondest father's fondest care
Can fashion so the infant heart.

– Landor

Romantic plays with happy endings are almost of necessity inferior in artistic value to true tragedies. Not, one would hope, simply because they end happily; happiness in itself is certainly not less beautiful than grief; but because a tragedy in its great moments can generally afford to be sincere, while romantic plays live in an atmosphere of ingenuity and make-believe.

– Gilbert Murray

When the third daughter declared that she loved him more than salt he flew into a rage.

– Brothers Grimm

Make not my father's house an house of merchandise.

– *John, II, 16*

1

IT SEEMED as unlikely as the venerable Shake-speare actor once dating a Supreme. Never having heard of him Greta was certain she *had* heard one or two Supremes songs. *"Baby love, my baby love . . ."* Teasing us, she laughed in her unruly way. "Is that the one?" I felt it better to say nothing more in case idle talk increased her willful attraction to this man four times her age and half her weight. If they were more than friends, neither Patrick nor I really wanted to know. A liaison like theirs might be plausible in a celebrity world of relaxed shack-ups, but to us it felt ridiculous.

"He's peacocking!" said Patrick.

We liked Rudy, it wasn't that we didn't. Even my parents had enjoyed his company, and we trusted him once to babysit Greta when our regular sitter had had a conflict. He melted her cheese bagel and dusted the den. At musical chairs she'd made him lift the needle off *Baby Beluga* so many

times he cricked his wrist. He waggled it, that evening upon our return, punctuating his account
of their time together getting acquainted. Like a
house on fire? Stop, I didn't ask. Before bed came
Princess Mouseskin—but he confessed she hadn't
settled until they played Chinese checkers on her
pillow. Although younger, two decades ago, our
old family friend was already balding and recently
into a comfortable retirement.

So no, it was not his lack of trustworthiness, at
least not quite. I was puzzled the next morning by
what I found on Greta's bedspread. His effect on
her felt coincidental. Yet imagining him now, bob-
bing up and down atop our daughter, who would
be unable to stop laughing at his effeteness, dis-
comfited us. Having to toilet him before she was
thirty could well turn her compulsive laughter
manic. She loved long swims, so it seemed gro-
tesque to contemplate for her an abridged future
of pre-palliative care. Patrick confided to me, and
I wished he hadn't, it would be like mating the
family's pet goat to a rubber raft. Shamefully then,
every time Rudy arrived that summer to take her
chopping carrots—once our front door closed,
and we watched him in the driveway ushering her
regally into his Nash Metropolitan, we fell apart on
the floor.

Howling?

We could as well have wept.

"Vintage slapstick," said Patrick. "He and that puddle-jumper!"

Her fullback bulk she inherited from her father. Until she turned nine, I had cooked leanly for them both, after which, when they wouldn't suspend their taco top-ups before bed, I gave in to more lamb roasts than were good for either. By fourteen she was approximately half her father's weight, and by nineteen all of it. By twenty I turned to Pacific cod and deluxe veggie burgers, too late to reconstitute her chronic hunger. I knew she was compensating on campus with oriental fare—just not of the Japanese variety. Pork, I guessed, not tuna—thick Shanghai noodles instead of sushi. Patrick had her tested for diabetes and an underactive thyroid, prescribed a statin for cholesterol, and made a valid attempt to put things right by yielding to a better regimen himself. He was unable to resist the snacks his clinic should not have provided its staff, but did, continuing to measure his own size between Important and Severe on the Body Mass Index, and so proving a poor model for the younger doctors, their patients, his own daughter.

Greta herself wondered about bariatric surgery to reduce the capacity of her abounding belly. Patrick poo-pooed this and checked her further for sleep apnea and atrial fibrillation.

A perfectionist about everything but her weight, she was sailing through college as she had through high school. Academically, that is. There she enjoyed snap quizzes as much as cryptic puzzles in the *Globe*. Do No Harm was the guiding motto of her current faculty, and if a challenging headwind blew up in her ethics course, her debating style was pointed and not always tactful. One evening over dinner at Pastis, she put it to us: "When could eliminating sodium chloride—you know, *completely*, from the food you serve—be called an act of love?"

"At McDonald's," said Patrick, "definitely."

She looked serious.

"Go on, sweetie."

He knew, from listening to patients, that it was sounder to establish a baseline than to answer any query too soon. A case history required forbearance, especially in ethical riddles of the heart, which Patrick was convinced this was, and not a practical question about blood pressure. Margaret claimed it was an interesting conundrum to imagine the consequences in a world of older men like Kim.

"Rudy?" I said.

"His taste buds," she explained, "have withered enough. Rudy's, yes. He looks like hunger on the heath."

Our Greta enjoyed her own sideshows. She was not the least ashamed of wearing activewear for plus-size people. *It Might Be Wise / To Acces-*

sorize. She herself would never have followed such chalkboard advice from a clothing shop we'd just walked past, one with svelte cubbyholes instead of counters for belts and scarves to pair with garb far daintier than hers. Her haircut looked like a boy's. She appreciated the athletic vigour of boys without ever attracting much male, or, for that matter, female desire. Whether she was as confident of her body as she appeared was moot. She was buttering a breadstick and burst into laughter. Our waiter hovered before being allowed to get in a word about his rabbit.

"I'm assuming," she went on importantly, "my word 'eliminating' refers here to the *entire* loss of salt, and not to an equivocal demise favoured by academics like my ethics prof. He's a bit of a joke. Hands-behind-his-head type." Relaxing into her assessment of his complacency. "He isn't hired to conjure hypotheticals that the real, afflicted world isn't likely to test or understand."

"Then I would have thought," said Patrick, "he was hired for the right reason."

I thought her hoot sounded unnecessarily aggressive. "... Maybe. But maybe the real world needs to be tested a little more capriciously?" She had avoided boring us, she said, with any of their predictable class debates about blood transfusions and assisted dying. Those "obvious, enlightened storylines" didn't offer much meat for debate. She'd conjured up this one herself to afford a more interesting exchange with her "enlightened, progressive 'parentals'." Like her father she enjoyed making outlandish equivalences—in this case, love and salt. But to us "parental units" her equivalence sounded a bit nonsensical. I couldn't help but think, having contrived to yoke herself to Rudy, she was challenging us to resolve our objection to a relationship that made little sense in the real world.

"A peculiar proposition," Patrick later agreed. Allowing, however, that in the real world of *affliction*—"Isn't that what she called it?"— their seeming friendship *might* enjoy a kind of logic.

Really?

Rudy threatened to step it up a notch, by taking her to a film.

Already, every Sunday afternoon, he was escorting her to the Living Room on Powell Street, a charitable act to help feed mentally challenged, often homeless men and women, inside a dedicated storefront of communal tables and an institutional kitchen. We could understand the rationale in this. Who could gainsay his generosity of spirit? Except you sensed his social responsibility wasn't going to exclude its *ir*responsibility should Greta's goodwill happen to connive with it when it came to changing his (inevitable) Depends and spoiling her future. "Are we maybe not getting ahead of ourselves?" ventured Patrick. (The same man who had recently floated the goat and raft equivalency!) Possibly we were, although it wasn't my conceit of the Old Vic actor and his pop singer that concerned me here. In that theatrical world, reliant on glamour and illusion, a couple convinces us of their compatibility when they manage to overcome our expectation of a natural order for couples. May/August acceptable; March/December is yoking it. Even an arranged marriage between Hindus has its safeguards against an unnatural alliance.

Given their disparity in age, shape, and promise we had no illusions about how the comedy between our own two glamourpusses would play out should it get to the stage of an "afflicted" world. *Death and Diapers* was not, as her father put it, the play Noel Coward wrote. He thought for a moment, before turning over to turn out the light.

"I prefer Noel Coward to Tchaikovsky," he said.

"Schubert."

"He was the down-to-earth guy, was he?"

"*Death and the Maiden.*"

"Ouch."

*

Rudy had been a practical man who'd made an excellent living from air conditioning. When he sold out, he had stopped playing golf—a sensible career move in my view, when business gab between holes is no longer the motive. But whatever acuity he once possessed, to rethink and then circumvent the need for freon—the strategy that enriched his bottom line—it now seemed to have dribbled away in his weakness for black-and-white reruns of *The Andy Griffith Show*. I recall him wryly asking us one evening if we ever caught these reruns. He smirked, squaring his narrow shoulders. "Shucks, Andy. I don't like to blow my own horn, but golly gee ..." Now that his younger voice had thinned, he did a convincing imitation of the foolish deputy Barney Fife, teasing us, waiting for Margaret to float down the banister in a crinoline. She didn't, of course. On the sofa he crossed his short, dwindling legs. We were watching *Jeopardy*, which he thought too buzzer-busy to take seriously the actual categories popping up on screen. His apparent fondness for sidekick sitcoms made it difficult for us in turn to take seriously his charitable side, no matter how many carrots he might chop.

Sensing our skepticism, Greta reassured us the next morning at breakfast that without his believing a word of the gospels Rudy was supporting an entire Union Gospel summer camp for welfare children. This alone had persuaded her to help him cook up vats of curry at the Living Room as part of the elderly Mom-and-Pop team from Gujarat, who followed the Baha'i faith and its stricture to offer comfort to the less fortunate in skid row. Patrick thought a touch of mania in Rudy's post-retirement devotion to the unfortunate couldn't be ruled out but he didn't mention this to Greta.

We wondered what other good deeds Rudy had in mind. We did not consider our daughter a charity, but perhaps he did, offering to squire her about that summer when her present life at college must have appeared as dateless as it had been in high school. He was a caring man, a solicitous man; it wasn't that. What it was, was that he was a *little old man with no future*.

Who did he think he was fooling?

Margaret maybe. Or else she was fooling herself, which only seemed to encourage his nobler instincts. She was now "seeing" someone, and although she would never portray it in this way, a teenage history of elimination at musical chairs could only have reminded her of never having "seen" anyone before. Beyond, that is, a recent med student in her immunology class, who mocked comics from his home province of Newfoundland, where he earnestly believed they were breeding by the bushel in every spud patch. Doing stand-up in our den, he was probably rehearsing his bit for fellow comics in the Student Union Building about a fat girlfriend. And, yes, there was the noodle chef at SUB whom we distrusted, not because of his dietary influence, bad enough, but because his intentions seemed perversely mattress-driven. He drove a van.

According to Greta, just friends.

Not until she and her friend Rudy started going out on what could now be considered dates—here a talk, there a doc—did we truly recognize the liability of Rudy's age. He had turned eighty-eight in June. A week or so later, they drove off for a day-hike to Garibaldi Lake. Margaret hooted brashly and told him he'd be lucky to reach lake-level without oxygen. Her skepticism helped to reassure us she saw him clearly for the age he was, for the agility or rather lack of it he actually possessed. He responded by claiming the volcano there hadn't erupted in ten thousand years. Worried, Rudy? "So," she later said to him, "what were you expecting, lava?" Halfway up the trail, already at an unfamiliar elevation, he had to be carried back down in a blanket sling by Greta and three hikers. He was that light—and then he wasn't. A thunderstorm, blowing down the valley, made his wet weight feel like a dead one. While she, unbalanced by her own weight, slapped at ticks.

No neurological damage, in spite of MRI evidence of past cortical erosion, yet the incident ought to have warned her of his growing tendency to push himself when the day of his *being* pushed—in a wheelchair—wasn't far off. "I think it's the parental units who are pushing it," she warned us. She was working this summer at Patrick's clinic, where I'd once managed the books, but just as often found myself booking appointments, filing records, ordering copy paper. Before our getting together, Patrick asked if I would ever consider giving up my position to help him raise baby Margaret and run his home. I'd watched him move like a fullback, graceful if hefty hips shifting shut the door of his examining room—and after a time said yes. The upgrade worked out for me, my older age no barrier to the two of us functioning well as a team, and I didn't mind volunteering at his golf club.

Where I had happened one day to reconnect with Rudy.

"Hello, Denise. Rudy Skupa."

I looked up from distributing name tags. This for a reception on behalf of a QC lawyer come to speak about stick-handling the proposed appropriation of the course when its lease expired down the road. "Rudy! How are you?" My tone exceeded whatever my feeling now was about Rudy, unresolved since cottage days. But I didn't, as my mother had, hold a grudge. I stood up smartly and offered him my hand.

He emerged later from the meeting to say he was going to cancel his tee-time. He didn't know how members could golf on unceded land in good conscience when it belonged to the Musqueam who lived nearby in crummy houses. The lawyer's strategy for holding onto its lease had gone unappreciated by Rudy. I assured him, when he asked, that my partner rarely golfed because of his practice. "Not another lawyer?" he wanted to know. "No, no. Physician. Just as billable." Over drinks in the lounge, studying his thinning hair, I was reminded of the summer he'd barged over with a generator that had given our cottage on Savary Island its first grid to run electric lights and a small freezer for the crab.

Magically, I remember, he crossed the new wires as if they were short-tempered garter snakes. He'd forgotten his snub-nosed pliers and made nifty do with our children's scissors. His hair in those days, when he had hair, was blonde, and my father said his voice resembled Dick Cavett's. "No, no," said my mother, over her record player that now had power. "Nabucco's." It wasn't quite what you expected, its richly modulated timbre emerging from a short man to create a large man's presence. If he chose to he could sound imperious. "How much do you still love me, Cynthia?" He was flirting with my mother, remembering a disagreement they'd once had about him smoking cigarettes, of which she sharply disapproved. "I could smoke punk wood if you like, from the beach?" He didn't mind putting himself forward when he thought he'd been forgiven. She felt that for a business fellow he had a distinct flair, calling the Irish-green sports shirt he put on for dinner, in place of his working wife-beater, "a wowser." She reserved judgment on his ashtray, when he remembered to use it, a small clamshell he'd found outside and placed atop the driftwood coffee table. It was casual at the cottage. I had noticed whenever he visited us in Babylon, as she referred that evening to the city, there were no ashtrays for either him or my father.

His tan face glowed that summer.

"Yes. I was in my bronze age, then."

I sometimes thought of asking him, after his disavowal of lawyers, to join us at home for a meal and decided to cold-call him a year or two later to see if he was free to babysit. I explained our emergency with Greta. "It's like old times," he said upon reentering the house. "Same bedroom?" He felt welcome after that evening to drop by in the same casual way he used to with my parents. He was a curious and congenial man, his off-the-wall questions allowing others to relax and trust—not exactly his charm, but his foursquare appeal. His voice had not yet lost its lower octaves, allowing it to turn wheezy enough in these later years to deputize. You could guess how he'd once made a success of his business if it meant courting, as it must have, the sort of building contractors who needed persuading of their need to recondition air in a temperate city. They didn't, of course, but he could be authoritative without sounding like the AC salesman he was. Patrick and I began to count on him as a reliable mixer at garden parties. I fully believed my parents, at least my father, had long ago come to terms with his tragic visit to the cottage. Apparently not so my mother. The last time he saw her, at her nursing home, she refused to see him. It had bothered Rudy.

Yet at her funeral.

"I'm sorry for your loss, Denise. Your mother should be canonized. I plan on petitioning her every day in heaven for the miracle of her zeppoli. Do you remember how she filled them with a honey concoction?" I didn't, no. "That she wouldn't divulge?" Alone in our kitchen once, he'd been sampling one of these pastries before she happened to introduce him to a hefty diva, whom he recalled was kind to him, very down to earth, when he hadn't felt comfortable mixing with the dressy crowd my mother had invited that evening to fete this soprano and her cast after their performance downtown. He said to me, at the funeral: "You'd been travelling, I remember. You were on top of the world, in pearls, enjoying yourself with everyone there. Anyhow, I was grateful to your mother for leaving us alone, the singer and me, shooting the breeze in your kitchen. She must have trusted me not to embarrass her, the lowly sales-man. Probably because she was from down under, she couldn't have been more salt-of-the-earth."

"Mother?"

"The singer. Your mother came from Saska-toon, right?" To memorialize her, he was finally going to butt out. "The least I can do. Atone for my intrusion at her party, and for much else. She pretended she'd forgiven me. I realize now she hadn't." Surrendered once, moral high ground for my mother was too fertile a position to abandon again. "We all like to feel aggrieved," suggested Rudy. "We're reluctant to give it up."

She had never been able to persuade my father, unlike Rudy, to give up cigarettes. Or pastries, which didn't appear to threaten Rudy, but whose sugar, amidst a gamut of other desserts, had even-tually brought down Daddy.

"I'm also planning to live longer," he added.

No one had ever expected to be asked back to Rudy's place and no one had been. As for any-one dropping by, as he himself liked to do at other homes, social etiquette seemed to require not embarrassing a bachelor in his own. Who knows, he might have welcomed a visit. He had lived by himself for decades in a large house with a peeka-boo view of the mountains and a bright copper kick-plate on its Haida-carved cedar front door. Patrick had driven past to drop off my casserole, along with a card to thank him for babysitting Greta. She had drawn him a chair, quite a fancy one with knobs, which he promptly called up to tell her he didn't deserve. She rabbited on to him about Princess Mouseskin. I refrained from mentioning the cigarette ash on her bedspread—a curious lapse on his part. I didn't think less of him, although I would have expected him to abide by a more astringent social etiquette than at home. He had just sold his business, having no family member we knew of who wanted to get his hands dirty installing air conditioners, even as the climate had begun to heat up and larger profits must've seemed, if not ripe for the picking, tempting.

*

When Patrick's ex-wife, Margaret's birth mother, got wind of an old coot dating our daughter, she drove down to Powell Street to see them in action herself. She believed the devil lurked in details and I suppose felt she was the person to exorcise him by paying more attention than Patrick and I to the nature of the rapport between the two of them. I suspect she was trying to impress Patrick. We would see Judy from time to time, not exactly the callous cougar you might expect in someone who preferred tennis players to fullbacks—yet one who'd been willing to give up her husband, as well as her daughter, for a tennis pro with a bulging forearm. She lasted two years on the Asian circuit with this wunderkind from Veracruz, before drifting back across the Pacific without him. No shame at all in sharing her photos from happier days abroad.

"Black, thickish hair, mussed up here on his backhand."

Living alone now, she seemed to believe the world still belonged to her, and assumed this included access to her daughter. Patrick, never quite over his cuckolding, agreed to her visits. I should have pushed back more. Began to suspect he was supporting her again, because she had no obvious income after returning from overseas—apart, that is, from a dress-designing sideline she aspired to profit from one day. Brazenly, from my point of view, he hired her as our babysitter. I made sure she did the laundry, hoping to discourage her willingness to show up in her fine natural fibres. Not to be put off, she would ask what I was feeding "Margie," appreciating that her ex-husband's genes probably had something to do with the child's cheeks shaking abundantly when she laughed—and, when she was older, her thighs from spreading noticeably across the sofa while watching *Lost*.

"She's getting very large, Denise. Her laugh's starting to sound like it needs a pill for the fits."

I asked Patrick if hysteria was what we used to call the fits. He supposed it was, but thought laughter in Greta's case acted as a sedative. "It's a harmless addiction, like core breathing."

"She's such a darling," said Judy. "Have you thought of stripes?"

She wasn't jealous of me, possibly because she never intended to be a mother and was grateful someone else had been willing to take on the job, freeing her up without guilt for more interesting pursuits than feeling responsible for "Margie's fits," or for anything else. Greta called her Judy, saving Mommy for me until she was ten, when we connected the triangle for her, after which she began calling me Mum and Judy "Joos." Never a moment of reproach, that I recall, nor had we come to expect one from a precocious child who expected none from us. Her once-removed relationship with Joos probably accounted for her willingness to tell *her* things she never told us. About her smoking—that had been news to Patrick and me. Judy persuaded her to ditch the habit if she ever hoped to attract a boy. It hadn't worked. Not that a date was the lubricant it had been in my day for social acceptance. Girls now went to proms by themselves and even slow-danced with each other. The only remaining stigma was the Sadie Hawkins Dance, if the boy you asked happened to decline your invitation. These days, I told Patrick, a choosier Dogpatch had probably contributed to the high rate of smoking recidivism among girls.

"I'll have to remember that when I prescribe Nicoderm. What's the dog patch?" Sometimes his quickness flies right past me.

The Living Room patrons' table manners were too much for Judy. "They hide their half-eaten plates and shout for seconds. Not just a few of them either, acting greedy. Nobody's all there . . . you can tell most of them are on meds." Reporting back to us she said Margaret and her "bosom buddy" delivered dinners from a stacked metal trolley, pushing it back to reload in the kitchen, before reemerging with butterscotch desserts.

"The pair of them act like Mother Theresa doling out mouth swabs to the dying. It's love-forty and they're serving one more hunger artist who can't return a thank-you. *Yet a dinner he gets!* Personally, I'd knock off his noggin'—or *her* noggin.'" One drug-skinny creature with henna-ed hair, we learned, had dumped her plate on the floor, screaming that vegans like Margie were Hindu people spreading diarrhea.

Judy wondered, though, if their teamwork really translated into couple-compatibility. "Like you and Patrick, *you* two never look like you don't belong together." She paused. "Afterwards, I noticed Margie in the kitchen scarfing down more than her share of leftovers while *he* scrubbed pots with the Baha'is. Not a lot of eye contact between them. They don't seem to share a wavelength."

Her reconnoitre had left Judy with a feeling that their "courtship" wasn't anything that was going to last. "Fools rush in, I guess. Does he have money?"

Adding, "He certainly has no buns to speak of."

*

One morning near the end of July I sniffed the first forest fire of summer. I was sitting in the gazebo. The province's dry interior was late blowing its smoke down passes to the coast this year. The redolence carried me back to a time of burning leaves, when outdoor fires were still legal and the city encouraged this manner of disposal instead of dump trucks. In those years, smouldering fires along curbs produced the same scent as wood fires from chimneys. Their smoke hung in the air through fall, braiding bare branches of elms and chestnuts in an ethereal haze. I still think of it as the smell of transience, conjuring up dead ancestors in carbon molecules stretching forward from wild forests to the present city's weed-free lawns. Time condensed to a blissful breath of smoke. Normally a smell that lifted me out of myself, like pungent seaweed or a whiff of club cigar, in spite of my resolve to become less nebulous.

This morning was different, the quality of ash not a mellow memento mori but a source of foreboding, so I took myself indoors. In Canada, where cremation smoke is scrubbed, it rises from a smattering of gas furnaces sanctioned by municipal decree— firewood isn't fed onto one of those outdoor pyres as it has been in India for millennia. Here, traces of carbonized human flesh aren't intended for public consumption, sparing an older woman like me, slowly losing her olfactory cells, from a reminder of the furnace door.

But cremation wasn't the smell, nor was it from a forest fire exactly. The radio said the smoke was coming from Burns Bog, adjacent to the city, an ancient scrubland underpinned by peat moss and liable to smoulder for months and even years if its fire wasn't dug up and soaked down.

Rudy, I thought, in a yoking as low-grade as any by Patrick—if Greta knew what she was getting into with his peat bog, she'd walk away before he collapsed again, leaving her to attend his lingering demise in a wrinkle of smoke.

A briny smell at the beach that evening reassured me. We watched her from the Showboat bleachers putting on her wetsuit. Not that we could spot her in the distance, among a hundred and fifty ocean swimmers. Her club welcomed all comers so long as the weaker among them towed a pink float warning stronger swimmers to give them room, or maybe, when they tired, offered something to grab onto as they bobbed for breath. We speculated about their pecking order as soon as the dark swarm of them dove in like penguins and thrashed the sea in pursuit of a lifeguard's rowboat along a string of buoys circling Kits Point in direction of the West End. Patrick said he was glad we'd started her off with swimming lessons as a child. Ironically, now, she would be one of the marathoners nearest the lifeboat with the least need of one. Slowly, thrashing, they disappeared from view.

"For a chubby," said Patrick, "I don't know where she gets the velocity."

"Not by towing Rudy, that's for sure."

"Unless he's floating atop her like a goat."

I slapped his shoulder to stop us howling again like lunatics.

There was a wait past sunset for the swimmers to circle back along the seawall to shore. Then another wait for the barge after dark to ignite China's contribution to our Celebration of Light, a smug euphemism to avoid any civic embarrassment of having to mention fire. We had come down early to secure seats for the fireworks. The bleachers were now full. You had to wonder why the world's greenest city, as we hoped to become, would invite to this bay every summer vast egressions of smoke from countries notorious for poor environmental hygiene and from others like Sweden who should know better. I suppose we hoped to soften if not incinerate our unofficial epithet

No-Fun City, lit underneath from erupting Roman candles, a vast pall of smoke draping downtown towers and enshrouding us all. Was leaf-burning, punishable by lethal injection, so much more toxic to our lungs than an atomic cloud?—than this ruinous disorder of a quarter million fun-loving folk, snacking on grapes and polluting shorelines, crowded into beery Bayliners, circulating overhead in Piper Cubs? All of these made it harder to breathe. Not so healthy either, E. coli, a high count of which had just been issued for the waters of two local beaches including this one. Offshore yachts pumping sewage, runoff from goose leavings, dogs with their own strand. Poor, forked creatures now officially enumerated as part of our own mess for the sake of explaining it away.

In their rubber suits and goggles the marathoners should also have worn mouth dams. The flooding tide had brought in a scum of apple cores and woodchips, bull kelp and beer-can webbings—and this evening, instead of grey-green the water looked brown, hinting at red tide. Greta for some reason preferred this open ocean to the more sensible surrogate of filtered seawater in the public pool's long shimmering lanes below us.

Surrogate for what, you wondered, the choppy real world? You imagined her equating *pool-swimming*, the subject of her favourite rant, with *an equivocal demise*. If she ever went down, she'd go down with guns blazing in her body-positive swimwear.

She joined us later in the gloaming, carrying her gear in an oblong hockey bag the size of a small coffin. She exploded into wild laughter.

"Did you see us?"

"Yes," lied Patrick.

"He drove it into the ocean. Out of the parking lot, around logs on the beach."

"Who?"

"Rudy."

"The Nash?"

"It's a boat too."

"I'll be," he said. "I do recall those harebrained ads from childhood. I think you could float a bug, too."

Volkswagen he meant. Maybe in a rain shower.

Excited, she spread out on our narrow bleacher. "Maiden launch ... well, *ocean* launch. Fifty years ago he said he sailed it in Skaha Lake."

"I'm surprised his chassis hasn't rusted out."

"An ATV cop ordered us ashore. He joked we needed sand tires. And then wrote us a ticket for operating a boat without a license."

"Rudy? He's lucky they didn't retire his driver's license."

Her hair was still wet. She had wedged her huge hips in beside her father's, the hockey bag now smothering her neighbour's lap. Patrick suggested

I sit between them to leave more room for the bag and to imperil her neighbour less. Greta said she was pretty sure she'd come fifth, behind three men and a woman, all of whom out-swam her by a furlong. They spoke French and were probably tri-athletes. We let on we'd spotted her, but hadn't really, as they all seemed to lift their arms in similar windmill mode to clobber the surface. A lot of roiling foam. "A lot of wake," said Patrick, the marathoner's stroke in his opinion not the most efficient. His barrel shape no longer attested to the compact efficiency of his own stroke, in the days he used to crawl up and down a lane at the Aquatic Centre before we hooked up. I went down once to watch him.

"Did you notice," she asked, "the infestation of Ski-Doos? They nearly swamped the guide boat." Her wild hoot in face of this averted calamity more than hinted at endorphins in full flood. They nearly swamped her neighbour.

*

We had felt for some time that such chemical highs helped lessen the associated risks of her obesity. Remarkable, given public intolerance these days for discarded butts and everywhere the clamorous enthusiasm for yoga studios, that her size wasn't more of an issue than it was. Patrick demurred. Since society was bending over backward lately for transgenders, he wouldn't be at all surprised to hear from some emeritus dean sipping sherry at his club that our daughter had got into medical school based solely on affirmative action. This irked him. That her admission—notwithstanding topnotch marks, which hadn't guaranteed admittance when every other candidate's were too—might have come down to no more than a minority quota for fat people.

"They have such quotas?"

"How do you think Rudy keeps his driver's license?"

I hoped it was because he was a careful driver, regardless of any age concession. I knew Patrick was already concerned about him driving Greta around in an antique cubicle. She was unable to strap its thinning seatbelt, a retro implant, the whole way across her midriff.

"Fat-shaming," he continued. "It's part of their ethics course now. *Is it permissible to mention weight loss to a fat person?* At the clinic I can't suggest to a patient he consider dieting unless *he* brings it up. And I'm a fattie myself! These days it's genetic propensity for weightiness we're expected to consider before mentioning unhealthy snacks devoured in front of Netflix." The acceptable was no longer acceptable. "Med school is no shoo-in even for *exceptional* applicants. In my day, it was more or less a shoo-in." In his day, he wasn't as fat as he is now, and he was a man. So I was glad of our new consideration of fat people, women in particular, although I would still welcome the smell of burning leaves.

The fireworks popped and whistled, screamed straight up and crackled sideways, bursting into constellations. Followed a second or two later by sonic booms. It was that night on our way home, too late to stop in at La Brass, and staring hungrily into the park overlooking hazy city lights, she mentioned she wouldn't be returning to med school in September. We waited. She was spread across the back seat with her wetsuit bag, like a homeless person. She then said she wanted to get some practical experience before committing to an internship in a comfortable family clinic like Daddy's. She hadn't called him this in years, so we knew she was joking.

"You don't intern in a clinic," Patrick reminded her. "The ER at St. Paul's will introduce you to enough fentanyl folks to last you a lifetime."

Perhaps, but she'd already been accepted by Doctors Without Borders, as an adjunct health worker, and she intended to embark this fall for Africa. What made her news more shocking was Rudy—he'd been accepted too. Classified a construction supervisor, he would be responsible for the camp's electrical plant and probably combustible latrines. She mentioned one of those bunched-up countries, where the fist of God had made it more or less inseparable from its neighbours along the Ivory Coast, where not one of them is immune to Ebola. We pressed for more positive information. Well, she responded, their contracts were not open-ended.

"What a bonus," remarked Patrick.

But neither were they non-transferrable.

"Hold on," he said. "You mean your tour of duty can be bounced about, if the risk in one country gives way to crisis in another?"

"I guess," said Greta.

Acquiring practical experience in this itinerant way was not the kind of acquisition parents wished to hear from their daughter—not when she could procure a good dose of practical specifics, as we did, every night from public television.

"I don't suppose you could choose Greece?" asked Patrick. "On Lesbos, it's mainly refugees." He was convinced countries in conflict, the sort favoured by Doctors Without Borders, left you ripe for the worst kind of misfortune.

She went silent. The darkened bowling green slipped by. I floundered for words to soften her father's disapproval. I hoped she would at least wear white. "Against the heat?"

"Leaf blowers of the sea," muttered Patrick.

I turned to him. "What?"

"Those Ski-Doos. You need ear muffs these days to plan a picnic."

Her laughter exploded like a galaxy, wave after wave bursting over us in echoes against the windshield, even after we thought her last boom had run out of powder and its ruinous disorder died back. We had to roll down our windows.

It helped to reassure us that if she wasn't in control of her future our Greta was able to see its bright side. This was our hope. Time would tell— or else I would. I wasn't going to let Judy have the last word, by any stretch.

"I can't get her to drop it," said Judy, "or to drop by." Judy lived in a subsidized flat in False Creek. So the two of them shared a long lunch at Au Comptoir, where Margaret ate freely of the mussels and said nothing to her to suggest she might change her mind and return to school. We had just shelled out a quarter million dollars for this year's textbooks, wondering now if their past-use date would lapse before she got back in time to use them. Patrick's own medical books were outdated not long after copper was discovered.

"Have you ever noticed how loud her laugh sounds at a zinc bar?" asked Judy. "It's getting wheezy. A pulmonologist might help."

Patrick thanked her for trying. He sounded more distracted than I remembered. I repaid Judy for the tab. The thought of his gifted daughter giving up medical training, while not exactly the case, was preying on him.

So too the smoke, he not knowing how best to counsel patients coming in complaining of sore throats, even of despondency, occasioned in this last half of August by hundreds of wildfires raging in the north half of the province and drifting south to sock us in day after day. Even I, normally stirred by such redolence, found the haze spectral. The sun at noon, once as yellow as a Giotto halo, resembled a small apricot, its watery light not a colour on sidewalks you recognized when filtered through leaves. Across the bay, islands and mountains offered only faint outlines—in truth, you couldn't see them. I walked down the hill carrying a hanky sprinkled with lavender oil against ground-level ozone. Face flags like mine were now plastering citizens of a new universal suffrage in favour of the Greens. Huddled Chinese families picnicked in the dead grass. A cool wind blew little tornadoes across the sand, where fewer than half the volleyball nets were strung out on the sparsely populated beach. I had heard the Adams River sockeye run was schooling around the point, gathering mass at the river's mouth, but doubted you could've spotted two gillnetters from the lowest-banking drone.

We didn't believe yet in her departure. Arriving to take her for their "last" visit to the Living Room, Rudy sat barking at Alex Trebek, immoderately jolly for a man supposedly on his way to the gallows in Sierra Leone. He pounced on the category of Good Sons and beat Patrick to the buzzer on every answer but one.

"What is Edmund!" called Patrick.

"Opie!" cried Rudy, late. Acting the fool, knowing full well he was wrong, just to give Patrick a bone.

"Gosh darn it," said Greta, descending the staircase in a chiffon dress with pink shoulder ribbons. Not, I guessed, a gown she was going to pack overseas nor one Judy would donate to a rummage sale. "You're just kidding him, Barney." And hooting something awful seemed determined not to sound at all like a college girl. Maybe never had. She resembled the Appalachia belle Daisy Scragg— although her "Barney" didn't look a bit like Ab Yokum, pole-tall blood enemy of the Scraggs and destined to marry their daughter. This was worse. We were living in a lapsed comic strip, the pair of them swapping caricatures whose merriment had long passed.

At least for us it had.

"Smarten up, Kim," she told him in the same village voice. "You let my father win that one 'cuz you want him to remember you for your kind, paternal side. You're no sharper than a geezer and you owe me a last supper out. And I don't mean kitchen leftovers."

What would the mentally challenged downtown make of this stoked pair serving them dinner like two loonies? Their intimacy had warmed considerably, if mock insults and pet names meant anything—calling her "Grit" on their way out, offering his arm, which she swatted at, suggesting they at least had one another's backs.

By mid-September, smoke suddenly gone, our March/December couple had embarked for the dark continent without her medical degree or his paying for the traffic violation on his amphibious car.

*

By the end of October we had an email at the clinic, where Patrick had asked me to come back and work after Margaret left. Her message informed us of her assignment to a team screening for malaria and HIV/Aids. Attached was a selfie, showing her neck wrapped in a bandanna of Sierra Leone's colours and her head, it looked like, in a crown of weeds. It looked weird. A video bearing a soundtrack of her crazy laugh might have better assured us she actually had the tropical sun under control. Rudy, she wrote, was going about his own business "unbonneted." If we thought *she* looked funny, we should see *him* covered in red dust from digging a midden for surgical waste. This in an interior district called Koinadugu, where as well as screening for diseases she was multi-tasking in the neonatal ward.

"I've lost some weight."

We heard nothing more of Rudy until learning, three weeks later, she hoped he would recover soon from a fever he'd come down with after collapsing while rigging up a generator-driven windstorm at the "rehabilitated" Kabala hospital to cool its operating theatre. Sunstroke, it sounded like. Holy cow, I said to Patrick. Hadn't the man been warned off his susceptibilities after climbing Mount Garibaldi? An incorrigible madman, it was now clear, talking himself into an African expedition and our Greta into joining him. Why hadn't we spoken out? As if all the Ebola ghosts weren't enough to haunt her future, he was the royal arse who would snatch it from her by commanding loyalty to his decaying presence. We liked Rudy, it wasn't that . . . well, in the end, it was that. We had begun to loathe him. Our original nightmare, unfolding.

An email in late November confirmed his worsening fever and suspected renal failure. The travesty of this philanthropic volunteer, scorched by his own hubris and now dribbling away. Followed by an Instagram post, showing not the patient but for some reason the image of a tourniquet, intended perhaps for a Swiss supplier and misaddressed.

"It's not the frontline for nothing," said Patrick. "Prepare for dengue, expect amputation."

Along with her other duties, she would now be up to her neck attending his decline. What if he survived but was too sick to transfer home—would she stick by him until he checked out? It didn't take much awareness of her stamina as a swimmer to know that once she found herself nursing him in palliative care she wouldn't request a transfer but would continue to carry on.

Her silence only confirmed this turn of events. Charity far in excess of what she'd volunteered for, akin to caring for a terminal Aids patient in a pup tent. Patrick began to let himself get carried away. Her intimate acts of kindness would be many, he thought, during Rudy's flagging trajectory. Her "contractual obligations" would loom even larger now in face of his personal withering. The pathos would be comic if it wasn't so pathetic. Changing his soiled diapers, spoon-feeding the fellow on a leaky air mattress, washing the drool from his white stubble after several days of not shaving his sunken cheeks—all this, continued Patrick, through difficulties involving possible Lassa fever, but more likely complications of peritonitis arising from an impacted bowel, enzymes from a malfunctioning pancreas, not to mention the aphasia that had descended to gibble his speech—a probable stroke he thought, notwithstanding the kidney failure, which would require rudimentary filtration of his blood once a day in an MSF shed to eliminate the creatinine he couldn't excrete naturally.

What a pickle. He liked to cover all the bases did Patrick. This was a case study he could prepare without notes. Taking dictation I'd have struggled to keep up. For our old friend Rudy, he concluded, it sounded like curtains. His normally skinny torso would now resemble a breadstick, his ... unlike Job, Rudy had lost his innocence and surely deserved his fate by misusing Greta. Her father's worst diagnosis? "Nihilistic nutter."

Our receptionist studied him through her new frames with the purple piping.

"Sorry, Lucille." Pause. "He's not a patient of ours."

No longer howling, at least not in the way we'd howled that summer while enjoying ourselves at his expense, we accepted the inevitability of Rudy's death. We couldn't say for sure it would not be from another deadly disease, equally tragic. Ebola, eliminated though not eradicated, was hiding in the forest. This was intelligence everyone had and no one credited until someone, either a native of the country or an itinerant health care provider, suddenly waned, slumped, died.

It was only a matter of time.

If Greta didn't die, she would become increasingly addicted to giving herself over to Rudy as *he* died. Her mandate, the mandate of doctors since Hippocrates, was do no harm. No less a charge, in avoiding any heroic intervention clear of easing Rudy's pain, was applying this dictum equally to herself.

"I don't have to guess," said Patrick. "I know from clinical experience elder disease can take its toll."

She was loyal to, if nothing else, her validation of adventure. Even by *dating* an old man our daughter had discovered an act to prove the risk she seemed willing to welcome. *A hypothetical the real, afflicted world was never likely to . . . etc.* In other words, yes, something of a joke. Cosmic joke? No, we should think of it as a career move, Patrick decided, since it had got her to Africa, where her breadth of experience would look good on an application to specialize, after she returned to her senses, in advanced geriatrics.

"Still, she could've carried on flirting hereabouts with gerontology and stayed in school."

A month later another email to say Rudy was dead. *He's gone. I'm not.* Relief—or grief? We were surprised he had lasted as long as he had, in a country like that one. Not a place for old men, you knew, or for that matter young women. Exhausted and eager to come home, she would now need to be released from her contract on compassionate grounds (we were confident of this) given what we were told by one of Patrick's young physicians, who had served time with the good doctors in Jordan—adding, though not in his finest doctorese, "The worst is not ... so long as she can say, 'This is the worst.'"

So at least that part of our nightmare was over, and possibly sooner than we expected. *R. Skupa, R.I.P.* Although we had admired Rudy's refusal to let himself molder as a retired clubbie, living off his golfing handicap and an RRIF, he had no business introducing our daughter to his irregular lifestyle before going completely bush.

Her own adventure over, a supreme corroboration of her worst hypothesis, she might now return to laughter and school. We waited in hope. When she got home we would certainly refrain from any *we-told-you-so's*.

And we did.

"Well then, I'll tell her," said Judy. "I never trusted her faith in him. She was dating the wrong end of the binoculars."

*

Early in his absence abroad we had driven by Rudy's house and noticed he'd rented it to a family, there were toys on the porch. We wondered what would happen to them now, this family, no doubt a disadvantaged one recommended to him by the Baha'is or maybe by a United Church acquaintance on behalf of Syrian refugees. Rudy might be resolute but he was also capricious, and this had had consequences. No one else drove his vehicle for a lark into the salt chuck, unless showing off to a girlfriend young enough to be his grandchild, whom he'd managed to charm or at least challenge with a dare, before he blew it all by dying ignobly. Not, said Patrick, the legacy he might have wanted.

"He made a good living out of air conditioning, only to suffocate her with his last gasps."

A twisted bike straddled the sidewalk and a long dog chain parted the uncut lawn. The flowerbeds looked neglected. As to the house, we'd never thought of Rudy as having an *heir*—so why, we casually wondered, might Margaret not be his choice? It would be compensation for her saving his life on Garibaldi and agreeing to accompany his liabilities abroad. At his age you didn't run away to darkness without considering the possibility of not coming home.

We expected her return within the month and I dusted her bedroom. Patrick said he had a patient we could call if and when it came to putting Rudy's realm on the market. This realtor could arrange to clean, landscape, and—should Mr. Skupa have failed to exorcise an old environmental ghost—to remove his buried oil tank. She would also employ a photographer, and, if needed, a Cantonese/Mandarin translator.

"Estate agents have become stage directors," said Patrick. "Your house is her production for the time it takes to sell. It wouldn't surprise me if she hires actors to talk up offers at the open. In this market, she probably won't need them."

He seemed unaware the market had cooled and that his patient was probably now fishing for any inventory that might attract families without an inheritance equal to one of the minor nobilities. Not that Rudy's house wouldn't attract deep pockets keen to clear it swiftly of all traces of Rudy's house.

Margaret stayed in Africa for another eight months. Never mentioning in emails her friend's last will and testament, or anything concerning the disposal of his remains. Knowing Rudy we supposed arrangements for his internment had been made before his departure—probably as far back as when he'd had his oil tank unburied—but we refrained from asking for fear of unsettling her at a time made worse by her poor choice of staying on. "I don't understand her," said Patrick, whenever we talked by telephone. "She always sounds so abrupt." I suggested maybe it was because she was busy attending deliveries of women with complicated uteruses.

"That's not quite how she put it," he said. "Are you this casual itemizing accounts of our expectant mothers?"

If anything, her experience abroad was toughening her up for the enervating grind of family medicine—far less exciting, he claimed, but just as draining as emergency care—once she got home and finished school.

She came back in August. We hadn't seen her since the previous summer, and, longing to welcome her at the airport, expected a wiser, well-seasoned young woman, her propensity for extreme charity and even extreme swimming chastened by her sobering exile from a perk like cinnamon buns, which she hadn't realized she missed.

"I'll just bring along this box from Solly's."

We were shocked though not surprised, given the ravages of frontline medicine, to see how much weight she had lost. Only her suitcase was heavier than we remembered, which we put down to an African cooking pot with doo-dad markings. Patrick thought it a wry souvenir of the so-so food she couldn't stomach and hadn't eaten. Dehydration, her anxiety over the dying Rudy, and a climate she'd mentioned in sporadic emails as either "un-redemptive" or "diabolical"—all such tribulations would winnow any overeater and help knock off the feeble. No longer obese, she wasn't even fat; her once chubby cheeks sagged when she smiled and wrinkled vertically. She did not look twenty-three. Her laugh had also changed; she'd lost it, or more correctly had lost the hysterical edge that used to relax, we felt, her angst incubated since adolescence by chronic obesity. This new laugh sounded a touch rehearsed. And she no longer burst into spontaneous song hoping to annoy us. Even speaking, she devoiced as if to echo her unfamiliar reticence.

"She sounds shell-shocked," said her father, "like she's still lost in the woods."

I was now trying to please her in a way I never had before, silly things, tracking down smoked salami and cream puffs. Pork chops and trashbean soup. I issued her a hunting license to buy Beefaroni. She was now free to binge in the way Oprah, until recently, had allowed herself to binge on cold ribs between meals. I would have served eight meals a day to plump her back up. At the PNE that month, a spontaneous distraction we hadn't suffered through since she was nine, I insisted we treat her to candy floss twirled from a glass sarcophagus fed on sugar. The cholesterol choice of angels, joked Patrick. He bought a bouffant cone for himself. She tongued the evanescence but its sweetness left her removed from any ensuing high.

"Sugar is all it is," said Patrick. "Gross sucrose." He was lapping at his with the furling tongue of a large lizard. "Not as tasty as a tater dog. Let's get her a candy apple. Fructose is healthier."

At home she nibbled at whatever she found on her plate and would barely finish a taco. It was not a matter of refusing something, but rather of never choosing anything. It began to seem everything was tasteless to her. "Malaise over mayonnaise," observed her disappointed father. She made few choices beyond flushing the toilet. We heard her flushing it a lot.

"Bulimia," he decided without consultation. "The purging sort." Circumstantial at best, this diagnosis lacked therapeutic or nutritional scrutiny to support it beyond his subjective impression of her appearance. That plus the frequent toilet. "I guess it's understandable," he said. "But good god, not *that*." This after a Sunday brunch at which we were tickled pink she had eaten a sausage.

Far from lifting, the cloud obscuring her future darkened further. Her father changed his tune and re-diagnosed anorexia nervosa based on her nearly total lack of appetite and indifference to exercise. "What happened to her swimming?" She had not submitted an application to return to medical school, and Patrick, beside himself, went on to speculate that if she *had* once gained admission on a fat-person's quota, a committee would now need to reconsider her eligibility on some new concession. He very much doubted there was a quota for ex-students with "anorex," so she would have to take her chances based solely on past high marks. "It's a shame, really. She should be a shoo-in."

But failing to reapply, when she might happily have rejoined her program a year late, *and* with estimable field experience, she was neither shooed-in nor reconsidered as a nervosa minority with affirmable but resolvable issues. Patrick called it a personal and social tragedy.

When the leaves turned in October, I was outside with a message to return his call. I had come home early to have a little talk with Greta and it hadn't gone well. I found her eating disorder, involving too little food instead of too much, difficult to broach. It was complicated by post-traumatic stress we could only guess at. In her room, where I had to knock several times, she volunteered nothing and told me to leave. No wonder. Having mentioned that the heart-shaped leaves falling outside her window lacked the drop-dead blush of our Japanese maples, thoughtlessly I called their colour "pukish." I felt like a douchebag. I needed to avoid mentioning sickness if I hoped to win her confidence.

"Listen," said Judy, "if she was puking, she'd be eating. She's not eating."

Judy had offered to help with what she started calling "the project," but I didn't feel it was Judy's right to do so when I was the one, not her, who had nourished Greta since age two. Until recently I'd been only too successful in feeding her, so her refusal now to eat anything more than a cornflake felt like a painful blowback from her fat years holding me accountable.

Standing in the garden I was on hold with Lucille. The length of my raking stroke had shortened up without my noticing until this autumn. A sore hip was also bringing a new me into focus.

"Are you sitting down?" Patrick's professional, understated voice was not entirely familiar. "The news isn't good."

A young female doctor at the clinic had confided to him that his daughter, Margaret Fitzgerald, might be buying drugs downtown. This colleague understood from her source—an unnamed patient who'd seen her more than once collaborating warily with a low-life on Powell Street—that such trysts, given Patrick's confirmation of Greta's arrival date, could have been going on since her return from Africa.

I took a moment to absorb our latest reconnaissance. The frequent flushing: possible cover for the sound of her snorting? Which might explain why the bathroom never smelled of vomit. At least, I replied, she wasn't smoking it. "Maybe not," said Patrick, "but she could be injecting it." He paused. "Heroin?" I squeezed my rake. *Really?* "Once or twice," he said, "I've smelt burning. Where there's smoke . . ." He mentioned a spoon. "No way," I said, "actual burning? I thought that was the hairdryer." Here was ammunition to confront her with when I returned indoors—drugs, house insurance, before long the fire alarm upstairs and a truck outside. *I'll talk to her again right away.* "Hold your horses," cautioned Patrick.

I decided it was his fault I'd spoken to her too soon. His diagnosis was based on a case history he had failed to establish. I replied that he should get his physician's act together, seriously, and document the nature and length of her addiction if we hoped to persuade her to seek treatment. This was the minimum we would need for admission to a recovery centre.

He considered this.

"A formal patient-physician sit-down, yup. But I doubt she'll come to the office. And we more or less know what happened." We did? "If we want her in rehab, sooner rather than later, I need her to agree she's addicted. That *she* wants help. We're past the diagnosis stage."

"But not beyond a case study," I reiterated. I suggested we reach out to doctors who might have known or worked with Greta at her clinic in Sierra Leone.

"No harm in that, I suppose. But we know enough already to get on with the antidote. Just don't involve Lucille."

"I thought the antidote was a treatment centre."

"It is, and the usual recipe there for recovery is talking therapy, plus methadone, when withdrawal sets in. She'll open up over time." He had recommended other patients for similar treatment. He thought her story of addiction, as she was likely to share it with fellow addicts, would in broad strokes go as follows.

This time he didn't seek to amuse me, as he'd done diagnosing Rudy's demise. Rudy had died of one malady or another no one treating him in the field would've had time to pinpoint before he passed. In Greta's case, Patrick was basing his "professional preview" upon other cases of addiction he had treated. What their substance abuse had in common was *access*.

"That's news?"

"No, but listen."

To alleviate her sorrow, after supervising Rudy's palliative care, it had been tempting for Margaret to sample the morphine his physician was administering to Rudy in his final days. She would've known where the drug was stored and the syringes used to inject it—inside a lockable cupboard to which she had sanctioned access or at minimum the knowledge of where its key was kept.

His confidence in this sketch was not surprising given his status among peers as a quick study. They'd given him the Fish or Cut Bait Award at an informal conference in Harrison for physicians and small pharma. Tolerating uncertainty counted, who'd discount caution?, but sometimes Patrick saw the picture whole before the patient herself could remember how or why she'd first fallen from the wagon.

Following Rudy's death, and with grief leaching Greta's determination to finish a full tour in Africa, he could see how, in the months following, an opiate taken for a pleasant release from pain had got her hooked and then had begun to dominate any determination to quit. Or to eat the way she used to. Indeed, proud of losing weight for the first time in her life, along with the flood of endorphins the drug afforded ("Didn't her swimming do this too?"), it was tempting for her to keep self-administering "pride" in this new, unexpected control over her body. "An illusion, of course." Yet here she was, rising above the excesses of appetite, and above the sad residue of her friend's death.

"For Greta it felt very good. And still does, unfortunately."

He brought home a naloxone kit and showed me how to use it. His clinic, while not a downtown clinic attended by welfare drug addicts, was seeing its share of fentanyl survivors among homeless youth.

"You can't be afraid to jab, the minute you find her."

On the floor he meant, as good as dead.

"She'll bounce back so fast she'll wonder why you're fussing over her."

That evening I came up with a veal hotpot to serve over couscous, and her demeanour, instead of scowling, looked non-judgmental for once, easing slowly to a smile as her father spoke frankly about administering morphine to Rudy as he died. I was surprised by the gentleness of his induction. He asked if perhaps she had been tempted to ease her difficult transition out of grief, and eventually out of a very difficult assignment in a hellish climate, *through the consolation of drugs now somewhat out of her control.* We happened to know, it didn't matter how, that she was still addicted to a sustaining substance, but we were, as her loving parents, here to help her get over this crippling habit.

When Patrick stopped she sat very still, on the edge, I thought, of tears she could barely restrain. And then her shoulders started to shake. She put down the fork she'd picked up. Catharsis, at last, some return to normality.

It took her a minute, finally, to explode into laughter. At what sounded like his entire premise. *Oh my god!* she shrieked. In convulsions, pushing away from her untouched dinner, storming upstairs. *You have no idea how annoying you are!* Her bedroom door, slamming. Not only had we not got anywhere, we were nowhere nearer understanding how she thought of her own emaciated

state. She opened the door to shout back down:
Why don't you stick to fucking Jeopardy?

"At least her laugh is back," Patrick said ruefully.

*

Greta's drug addiction came as a surprise to Judy.
I was pleased to see how far out of the loop she'd
drifted. She nevertheless felt—a week later, when
she dropped in for a glass of wine, wearing a pol-
ka-dot blouse that didn't suit her—that Patrick
had possibly gone about confronting the issue in
the wrong way and she left promising to figure out
a better way. She would start by inviting Margie,
her pet name still grated on me, for a hit of double
espresso and a girlie talk. She was determined to
be a better mother.

"Sorry, Denise. But I am."

Her presumption that she was her mother
at all pained me. Also upsetting, somehow pre-
suming she had the inside track to our daughter's
confidence, while remaining ignorant of my own
inquiries into Greta's doings abroad and lately her
domestic ones. Where was she getting the cash to
indulge her habit? From a dwindling stipend
via the good doctors in exile? Perhaps, but I was
still monitoring our household treasury, starting
with the silverware, just in case the resilience of
her virtue had suffered along with her health since

its decline abroad. I checked for figurines missing above the fireplace and the waffle maker. The walls for minor Smiths and Onleys. Proceeding upstairs to any space emptied of Hockney or a Shadbolt. If things were missing, and I sensed they were, I wondered if I wasn't hallucinating. I wondered about the essence of addiction and, opening the lid of my jewelry box, the riddle it now occasioned.

I confronted Patrick.

"Listen to me, all right? If two of the three virtues were eliminated—entirely—which one remains to equal love?"

Patrick looked at me, a little surprised at the span of my distraction. "Are you using, too?" he joked.

He wasn't inclined to answer, until I told him my opera pearls were missing. As a girl guide I'd played the Jewel Game, to remember which stones had been removed, so the pearls were easy to see gone.

"Charity?" he now answered. He seemed wary there might be something else missing.

"I wonder if that's true, Dr. Fitzgerald." I lifted my hands, parting them in a benevolent manner. "Faith, hope, charity—isn't the greatest of these *hope?*"

Interest in his apple strudel increased noticeably.

I said, "Without hope she's got nothing."

A little sarcastically, he responded. "And nothing comes of nothing?"

I considered how to answer this. "With nothing to look forward to, yes. Apart from a rush, always dissolving to despair, how can she be faithful to the future let alone to herself? She certainly can't be *charitable* to herself. Or forgiving of her past mistake."

I was struck by my persistence. Patrick finished his dessert and tabled his spoon.

"And selling off pieces of her home, for another fix, keeps hope alive?"

"Can you blame her?"

" Depends. My good cufflinks still around?"

"Patrick, we are talking about the extinction of her life. She could be suicidal."

"Hm."

I wanted this to sink in. "Unless she remembers what it's like to be hungry, she can't yearn for much besides drugs."

Nodding slowly, he lifted his napkin and wiped his chin. I was only furthering his case study . . . this one of *me*, his bookkeeper and homemaker, not previously known to him as an ethical whiz woman.

I confess the feeling pleased me. Over a decade older than Patrick—my perspective widening a little every year despite shrinking telomeres and silver hair, recently the glimpse of a withered underarm reaching to turn off my bed lamp—I still might surprise him enough to rehabilitate his unspoken regret of having once lost the industrially breasted Judy to a tennis tramp. With Judy, she always seemed a touch too eager to hear her out, over what was seldom worth reporting. I'd never expected him to marry me, and it didn't matter that he hadn't, but I did want to be appreciated as someone capable of framing case histories of her own, including, I thought, one of *him*. It would frankly run along the lines of many men's remotion, women's too, should age threaten not to resolve some past shame when the need to withdraw sends us wandering. Except in Patrick's case, the opposite was true. He enjoyed his work and the thought of travel only made him yearn for one more colleague to expand his clinic. His was a *family* clinic and he was loyal to its growth.

Not until the following Saturday did I have something more dramatic to report than pearls. At our door had come three measured knocks. Standing, a policeman, chirpy with static from his two-way radio clipped to a black, pen-spiked shirt.

I was eager to share the purpose of his visit with Patrick. But Judy dropped by with her own news as soon as he returned home from the office. She was reporting on her meeting over coffee with Margie "to talk turkey"—not, she regretted, as in "cold turkey," but enough turkey to persuade a grateful Patrick that, along with what we already knew, it might help to complete his case file for her recovery.

"Yes," said Judy smugly. "It was kind of a catharsis for her. Finally dealing with the old fool's ashes."

Ashes, what ashes?

"The ones she and I set free in a cloud at low tide. Yesterday, at Spanish Banks?"

"Now we're getting somewhere," said Patrick. "Out of the cooking pot into the ether. I guess we spotted his ashes without knowing it at the airport. What else did you find out, Joos?" He sounded mirthful, and apologized. "No, his deathbed can't have been a happy time for Margaret. Caring for him, no way."

"What deathbed?" asked Judy.

In her rush to tell us of helping to pilot his ashes to their final resting place, surely a misnomer at low tide, she had clearly forgotten the details of his death we'd shared with her months ago. It felt good to underscore this by reminding her of something *else* she didn't know, and that Patrick didn't either.

The tall young constable at the door had asked me about Rudy's Nash Metropolitan. Parked for a year in his garage, it had been stolen and found for sale on Craigslist. When the constable removed his cap to share this unexpected news, I noticed his hair was kinked by nature, certainly not shorn regimentally, a chestnut tint women other than myself only hoped to emulate. "Oh, get on with it," said Judy. Well, I continued, the current Craigslist "owner" off Renfrew had confessed to this constable that, yes, he was now reselling it—he had bought it originally, also on Craigslist, from a very thin woman who said she was selling it for her grandfather. I was then asked to identify this woman who had sold the vintage vehicle to its new owner for a song. He had found Greta's expired student card in his lobby.

I was pleased to see I now had Patrick's undivided attention.

"Well," replied Judy, "maybe she felt entitled to at least his car."

"No," I said. "She didn't. The more entitled she feels—the closer she comes to *this*."

And I pulled down from the kitchen cupboard, where I kept it handy in the colander, the naloxone kit.

"What is it?" asked Judy.

Patiently, I unzipped it and began to explain its purpose. Removing the blue non-latex gloves, I pointed out swabs, a pair of syringes, three vials of naloxone, a plastic mouth-to-mouth piece to blow oxygen into Greta's brain if her breathing stopped. I could see Patrick was impressed by how carefully I'd taken responsibility for our daughter's survival in case of an overdose at home.

"Into muscle," I said to him, "not a vein. Blue lips and nails, that means—"

"Well," interrupted Judy. "Whatever it takes, I guess." Studying me a little sadly, seeming to doubt my intervention would be required. She was reluctant to buy into any drug theory that lacked symptoms she herself had observed. "Anyway," turning back to Patrick, "there wasn't any death-bed. I don't know where you got that notion."

"Her palliative care," I said, hoping to hold my advantage and get back to the policeman.

"Not what *she* told me ..."

Not a volley Patrick could ignore. Rudy's ashes had been a bombshell. Further reverberations couldn't be ruled out. The upward cast of his brow told me he thought she might have something else we weren't privy to but badly needed to know. He turned to me.

"Judy seems to have tapped into the mother-daughter thing."

"Really?"

I told him to henceforth stick it where the sun no longer shone.

I didn't tell him anything. I knew based on what he'd long chosen to remember as "Judy's heartbreak overseas"—after her tennis hotshot had deserted her for a Japanese geisha, or was it another player's partner?—that he felt she could empathize with

Greta's experience in a way as to elicit confidences he and I could not.

Turning, I said, "What did our Margie tell *you*, Judy?"

"Well, for one thing," she replied, "the house. He offered it to her."

"We expected as much." I was more confident now of our deduction. "His legacy will help compensate for what she's missed out on, abandoning school and friends."

"He was her only friend," Judy reminded us. But agreed it made sense for him to bequeath her something more than anguish—after indulging the fool as if she'd had nothing better to do than follow his charitable obsession to the dark continent.

"Yes," repeated Judy, "it would've made sense if she'd accepted it."

"The house?"

"She refused it."

"The house," said Patrick.

"Go figure, yeah."

"Trying to," he said, shaking his head.

"He even told her," said Judy, "if she refused it, it would end up with his least favourite daughter."

Daughter? I decided she was now willing to say anything to keep Patrick enthralled by this mother-daughter thing she suddenly had going with him.

She went on, "He told her that *she—Margie—* was his favourite. I don't think he meant a charity, either."

I had to think for a moment. But the echo persisted. "If you're talking about a *daughter*, I wonder if he wasn't talking about a banquet? Rudy liked fairytales. With Greta, you missed out on a lot of those."

She ignored this. "I'll talk to her about the Nash."

"Greta?"

"Rudy's daughter. I'll pop by."

"Well," I said. "Let her know there's an overdue traffic violation on it. They've *impounded* the vehicle."

Before leaving she made a point of returning to his deathbed. To our apparent *delusion* about his deathbed. ". . . I think you're wrong there. At least where Margie's concerned. She's said nothing about a deathbed."

Patrick looked puzzled. Still sitting at the kitchen island after she left he slid his glass across the granite. I was washing out the wine glasses.

"She'll say anything," I said.

"Who, Greta?"

"Her too."

He picked up the empty Merlot bottle and took a swig. "Obviously, Judy being Judy, she favours drama-queen stories that remind her of running off to her own Timbuktu." He was trying to make me feel better. "Don't know why she can't open up to *us* . . ." Margaret, he meant. "There had to be a deathbed. They spread his damn ashes."

The following week I heard back from the Swiss office of MSF. They were sorry for our loss. (I had been careful to state in my inquiry that Mr. Skupa was part of our family.) The response was not at all what we'd surmised about his death. Even Judy's deathbed intelligence had been at best half-baked. I wanted her to recognize this at the same time I reported the facts to Patrick.

I reported them over dinner.

Rudy, it seemed, had requested a transfer soon after arriving in Sierra Leone. The office in Switzerland did not know why, except his re-application suggested that his experience in silviculture might be better utilized in Niger. *Silviculture?* When glaciers receded, had he once nursed seedlings? We knew him only as a wire and cooler guy. The office person, a Scandinavian by the sound of his noir accent, went on in an even, professional voice. Mr. Skupa was eventually sent to plant acacias in semi-arid holdings that grew peanuts.

"Peanuts," said Patrick.

I shared this intel about Rudy's peanuts, or rather his contribution to the future yield of peanuts. His expected contribution. Peanuts were grown to make something called Pumpy'Nut, a paste fed to malnourished children in the feeding centre Mr. Skupa had reached from Sierra Leone. His trees were to help conserve the necessary top-soil for growing the peanuts.

The man who called had regretted to inform me that Mr. Skupa had lost his life shortly after arriving in Niger.

"Niger," repeated Patrick.

"Apparently, yes. He was hired as a 'remote camp manager' to oversee trees."

This news must have suggested to Patrick how far his own case history of Margaret's addiction to drugs had now eroded into a handy but dispos-able fiction.

"*Trees*," he repeated. "At his age, the triumph of hope over endurance."

*

"Anything else?" asked Judy. I had been careful to get her on speaker-phone before sharing my news from MSF with Patrick. "Denise?" She was listen-ing in as I served him his dinner.

A pause was important here to savour my advantage. I poured the wine, ringing slightly the bottle's neck against our crystal glasses.

"There is, yes," I now answered. I waited for Patrick to lift his glass. "Here's to Rudy," I said. We both sipped. "Rudy," I explained, "was killed one morning in Maradi for his cell phone. At least as far as my MSF contact can confirm it, that's what happened. A suspected rogue member of Boko Haram shot him in the head."

Patrick looked shaken—I mean, shaken for a physician long used to the drama of life and death. He set down his fish fork. He had eased my own father into death, the resolution to what Daddy had long called his "tricky ticker," some years before it was legal to do so with morphine injections.

"The pathos," he finally said. "A fool like him, going off to die in the barrens of Niger—for what? *Charity?* For nothing."

"Nobility, I suppose." Judy's voice through the receiver sounded reassuringly thin. "Margie didn't mention *how* he died. If she was even told."

Margaret we believed was in her bedroom. She had refused dinner, arriving home that afternoon more tired than usual, muttering to herself that the downtown library was a "flu pit." She dumped a book on the foyer bench, sneezed, and vanished upstairs.

"All she told me," said Judy, "was he passed unexpectedly. When we were at the beach."

She decided to go on. The ashes they were pitching into the ocean breeze had blown back in their faces. She herself had had to turn sideways. But Margie seemed to welcome the chance to renew her grief, speaking hesitantly between handfuls of what Judy called "Rudy's last fling."

"No pangs worse than grief, I guess." She was wondering how to upstage me. "Unless it's child-birth?"

Her voice sounded small against the oak where I'd placed the phone in the centre of our dining table. I was satisfied to keep her at a distance, making the resurgent "mother-daughter thing" harder to sustain. Besides, I had the scoop, so there wasn't much more for her to tell us.

"Yeah," said Judy. "She really spilled the beans."

Patrick raised his hand to silence me. Arrested in mid-air, the glass in his other hand, head now inclined toward the handset. "Go on?"

"Rickety Rudyard," she now called him, "left our daughter, not long after suffering sunstroke in Sierra Leone. I'd forgotten how he'd crumpled up on her, climbing to Garibaldi Lake." Vigorous at first, he'd erected compostable latrines with fans he wired himself, and ordered local woodchips laid down inside toilets to help absorb the waste. Fellow aid workers had indulged his interest in helping them with laptops and hairdryers connected to the wrong kinds of plugs.

"I can just see him, poking his nose into the local sockets."

She was enjoying this, milking his tragedy. I suspected most of it was fabrication on a pattern sketched faintly for her by Greta. Still flirting with her design line, Judy, knowing where the zipper went, how the sleeves attached, and the kind of cuff to stitch, was dressing up Greta's pathetic story. His *official* reason for a transfer was that his expertise could be better utilized in a less-developed MSF clinic, "...in Niger, you now tell me? *But*, according to Margie, that was just an excuse on his part. To set her free."

"Free?" Patrick said. "Chained to African diseases without Netflix?"

"At least he was no poltroon," said Judy. "Flawed, maybe."

Nodding, we pretended to remember what "poltroon" meant. Probably no worse than a goat. Judy thought removing himself deeper into the boonies must have challenged Rudy's sanity.

"I think it challenged Margie's," she said. "The abrupt news of his death? That'd give even Mother Theresa the black dogs. She hardly had time to say good-bye and *bam*. The thing that defeated her," said Judy, "and still has her in its teeth—he'd let her think she was spicing up his life..."

"Well, wasn't she?"

I didn't know if she heard me, standing at the sideboard now with Patrick's plate, about to ladle his stew. Venison chunks in port sauce, prefaced by a pan-fried herring in bacon rendering, to be followed by a whipped pear mousse. A happy autumnal variation on his usual fare of lamb and mashed, which kept him girthy but not always satisfied.

"Actually no, Denise," said Judy. "He'd agreed to accompany *her* to Africa. Margie got a bee in her bonnet about helping out in a wider world than just the Living Room."

"That's odd," said Patrick. "We offered to send her to work with Jimmy Carter. House-building. She could've got it out of her system the following summer."

"The thing though is this, Patrick . . ." Her telephone voice starting to sound winsome. "His transfer? The real reason? He hadn't wanted to burden her with having to look out for him in case he collapsed again."

"Nobility?" said Patrick.

"Shame," said Judy. "On her part."

She didn't like to say, and was only repeating what she was told, but Margie realized Rudy's silent arrangement to unburden her of himself must have begun a day or so after she'd laughingly repeated to him, not long after their arrival in Sierra Leone, what we—"and more especially *you*, Denise"—had once remarked about her dating a geriatric with whom she'd soon find herself bogged down, nursing him through skin and bone to his last rattle.

Patrick glanced back at the speaker-phone, then at me. Vigorously, I shook my head.

"Rubbish," I said coolly. "I've never said anything of the sort."

Not to Margaret, anyway. And nothing corresponding to this gaunt analogy of Judy's. It also hurt that Greta might have called me *Denise*. Especially to Judy.

"Maybe he finally figured it out for himself," I said. Removing Patrick's fish plate and setting down his stew.

"Indeed," agreed Patrick. "Ricky was a whimsical fellow. He could act bizarrely. Isn't his house still a mystery?"

"Indeed," I said. And turning toward the phone, raised my voice. "We thought you were following up on his daughter, his so-called daughter, living there? After we last spoke?"

"I'm planning to," replied Judy, defensively.

"Ah," I said. "But weren't you the one hurrying down like a dizzy Sally to check out Greta—at the Living Room—before she could say uncle?"

"That's your characterization. Did you also tell her Rudy was to blame for your brother's death?"

I lifted the handset from the table and pressed Off. Smiling, I sat down to my own plate and then stood up again.

We both waited to hear if our daughter might be listening from upstairs. Going to the bottom of the staircase, hoping she'd change her mind and

join us, I noticed her library book was a copy of
BC Health Guide, which you could only pick up at
a drugstore.

This was not nothing I thought.

*

Judy soon found out that the present occupant was
not interested in the return of the Nash Metropolitan. Hadn't realized it was missing from her garage.
Had never been inside her garage. She wasn't interested in pressing charges against Margaret or in
paying off the outstanding ticket and impound-
ment fee. She had pointed out to the police that
they couldn't have legally issued a fine anyway,
not for a boating infraction in federal waters. "The
chutputz!" remarked Judy. She complained to Judy
the police would be returning the vehicle—minus,
for some reason, its convertible hardtop. How
could she sell it now? While the probate advanced,
her executor's powers would allow her to continue living in the house before she got rid of it.
The Nash she meant. She intended to stay in the
house. She had someone's grandchildren living
with her, but didn't say whose. Hers maybe.

Judy had come by to fill us in on the house
that ought to have gone to Greta. She was wearing
shoulder pads, a power suit of excessive expectation for such a modest invitation from us, but it

was probably what she'd put on to impress Rudy's "least favourite" daughter when she called.

Margaret was upstairs, refusing again to come down for dinner. This had been going on for weeks. Possibly a gerbil-bit of lunch, then nothing before the sound of flushing. We remained on tenterhooks, sniffing for burned air. Then Patrick would drive back to the clinic.

"Are you still insisting on the rehab route?" asked Judy, savouring my pâté.

Patrick said he was referring her to a nearby recovery centre called The Orchard. Detox was expensive. Still, there was a wait list.

Judy claimed Rudy had actively disliked his daughter. Margie told her this woman had never given him much comfort. Fostered as a teenager through Catholic Charities, she hadn't lived with him for more than a year before running away to the States. In later decades, through two marriages to deadbeat musicians, she'd badgered him for money. Studio productions gone sour, her children to weed, a persistent reliance on food stamps. She'd made it for a time as a minor pop singer, but had grown gradually blowsy, returning recently from a tinder landscape and a felony charge for growing domestic pot in Fresno, California.

"Caali-fornni-caation. . . !" sang Judy.

This fabrication was getting away from her. Greta had no more told her all this than a barn owl.

"You should've asked her if she ever sang *Stop, In the Name of Love*. She's probably Diana Ross's age. Has Greta met her?"

"She already has enough on her plate."

"The point I guess *is*," I replied, adding rosemary to my roast, "she never has *anything* on her plate she's willing to *eat*."

Patrick smiled. I was going to have the last word, whether Judy liked it or not.

"Her weight, yes," said Judy. "It's a worry for you both. The way it never used to be—when she was so fat? I used to worry about my own weight. I thought about my ass more than was healthy."

Now that she had the stage, she allowed the wine to divert her. She said in Tokyo she'd had lots of time to study girls in tennis skirts. Uninterested in seeds, she had nothing better to do during tournaments than conclude that a woman's progress, far more than a gentleman's, could be marked by her behind. Competitive in its own way, an expanding continuum, from youth through middle-age, "roughly"—she went on—"ass, bum, bottom, rump." *Ruummp* she called it, with resigned finality. Not, she added, the progress of *all* women, while nodding generously, I thought, in my direction.

If thanking me for the invitation to dinner, it felt more like an excuse to carry on. It was rare, she continued, but a defining shape was sometimes settled into for good at an early stage and her lover learned over time to be grateful for this contravention of the genetic time machine. She wondered if Patrick appreciated what he had in me. Something, she confessed, her own machine had missed out on—"any arrest of the natural progress."

"I'll admit these days, I'm somewhere between bum and bottom. When Patrick first got hold of me, I was early bum. Late ass, maybe. I was probably never in the nice-buns category, but relatively few girls are—not like you were, Denise, always slim—or if they are, don't last there long. Rafael, it turned out, preferred buns. Avocadoes, the Mexicans call them. Or used to, *agucates.*"

She spread herself more pâté before following me into the dining room. We could have done without this wandering monologue, but it amused Patrick. So I've left it in. Lips followed a pattern opposite to bums. "Plump to shrunk," she said. "The long thin bias, upper one a downer when it starts to shrivel." Body-image blether, I thought, of the sort unworthy of anyone's case history, including her own. Her story was an open book but hardly worth reading. Abandoning a *baby* for the gratification of her own body? I knew I could never really respect Judy and began to resent setting out a fourth napkin, the chandelier picking out my fingers now crawling stubbornly across the table to pull a fresh glass into place.

My mother had loved this wide stage of polished oak. A heritage table of hers and my father's, which had entertained its share of industrial lieutenants, even Rudy, capital builders of an emerging province. I intended to leave it with the house if Greta didn't want it—if she decided not to, or couldn't have sixteen children—as it would be too long to fit a modern dining room, and you couldn't flog it on Craigslist unless to a boutique sawmill for repurposed old-growth dining on smaller tables inside shoeboxes.

"Our Margie went from muffins to cake in the short span of childhood, Denise." This lament should have passed as well-intentioned collusion. But looking right at me, from the chair where she'd plunked herself, halfway toward Patrick's, she said: "Suddenly, in the blink of a year, she's entered the old-lady class with no buns at all."

You had to wonder why she bothered to compliment me in the first place.

2

DOWNHILL, a workout for my thighs from holding back on the forest path. Across Marine Drive
and around logs to low tide, stones sloping slickly
into kelp, then plodding onward through mud to
these rumpled salt flats stretching seaward a mile.

A trapped channel of saltwater, its wind-driven
wrinkles lapping at the silos of my gumboots. A
shock of cold in the left one before, squelching, I
reach a sandbar. This association of a dry sock and
a wet sock, otherwise identical, making me receptive to how memory can double-dip, how it can
trick you into thinking the serpent has slipped out
of a second cuff before you realize, as I would this
morning, that you've seen it do so only once. Every
memory you suppose being a magic trick, its construction a reconstruction of what has been, for
the most part, lost in time. Like this chronic poppy,
the same one pinned to the lapel of my peacoat, a
duplicate for decades. I should be ashamed.

Tide pools shot by crabs no bigger than shrapnel. In my face, the November breeze, and as part of its molecular brininess, Rudy Redux, his ashes leaching deeper into the sand, and floating up from clam holes where they've drained since his reported dispersal. Herring gulls. A clamshell. Across the blue bay, lying in mist like an etherized patient, the island and our exiled daughter until recently resident in its bosky retreat. Getting cleaner by the week, we earnestly hoped, hungrier too. Physician, heal thyself—unfortunately, not an option for Greta without help from the island's good people, caring people. A small white ferry tracking its coastline, headed to the gulf.

O bring back, bring back...

The breeze, yes. Rudy had lived by recycling hot air—returning it cooler, fresher—and died lying in some dusty back street of a searing country. Must have wondered why his sacrifice for "Grit's" sake had come down in his final moment of exile to nothing more than madness, treachery. Or did he envision, in a second of stopped time, being borne back to a happy little kingdom of collectible cars and charitable acts on currents of air and ocean? His briefest memory of being murdered had to be his most vivid, bursting into death with an awareness that escaped him bursting from the womb. Ninety years recirculating in a single round to the temple.

A wet sensation extending upwards through my hips. Recollection of his trauma bearing me back to the time of my vulnerable self. His ashes making me think of the woman I, too, like our daughter, had wanted to become. "Self-love," encouraged the therapist, "is recoverable." We were interviewing her at The Orchard pending Greta's admission. My own story, not just our daughter's, part of the case to be made in accounting for Rudy's exile.

My mother had been furious when she noticed my bedspread the next morning. It was not thought so much a crime when I was a child, or even talked about when it happened around children, compared to two generations later, when children were taught to stand up for themselves and say no. Less evidence is now required, about any transgression, to sustain or even suggest culpability. I was happy when my father came into the room after Rudy left. He sometimes did, to tuck me in. Emotionally distant, though not quite so removed as my mother, he sat on the bed breathing a little heavily and said he was "played out"—I guessed from golfing too long that afternoon with his "tricky ticker." He smelled of tobacco, of himself. I wanted to finger his thinning crown, and for him to forgive me for not finding his presence as rousing as Mr. Skupa's. He couldn't make-believe in the same way.

My ardor surprised him. "He's left you over-excited. Give me your hand." He began to rub it. As a five-year-old, I felt sorry for him. "The sun," he said, "has turned your hair golden."

Rudy's generation was the dubious beneficiary of my father's. All of them smoked as a rite of passage, continuing to inhale during life's remaining cruise through health and sickness until they disembarked with cases of emphysema, polluted arteries, lung cancer. Daddy, an electrical wholesaler, had got to know the younger Rudy through building contractors they had in common. My grandfather had sold wire and cable to municipalities and builders in the growing towns of British Columbia—before my father, after getting into dishwashers, TVs, turntables, recommitted Catalpa Electric to construction supplies, including the air conditioners he invoiced to Rudy. He died still totting up figures my mother mockingly called his "jolly numbers"—while Rudy, failing to believe in his own indispensability, had the later good sense to retire before his business retired him.

When I first knew Rudy, he had been around since the Middle Ages with its castles and serfs. He couldn't have been more than twenty-five. I suspect my mother had asked him as a favour to babysit when our nanny was visiting her family in Ecuador. The same way, decades later, when Judy couldn't come, I needed someone we could trust to sit Greta. Someone cheerful who liked children. Rudy was someone without family obligations and available to accommodate those of others, including dogs and offspring. This at least was the impression he gave, the affability of a confidence man you were confident was not one.

When my mother began rebuking my father over breakfast—not wanting them to quarrel, I said it had been Rudy. Theirs was a mock-bicker mode of a marriage, yet one likely to endure for the benefit of some estate plan after papers were sealed and mailed back to a law firm with signatures and reimbursement of an invoice. My father respected invoices. Marriage was less cut and credible. Marriage hadn't helped him all that much, I supposed, from feeling "played out." He had endured enough of my mother's nagging without having to answer this morning for the "shocking lack of respect" he'd shown his little girl the night before.

She studied me atop my big-girl booster seat at the dining table. And then promptly disappeared to call Rudy, to condemn his unconscionable conduct. She used our telephone on the wall inside a little grotto in the echoing foyer. *"Alma 3090-L!"* My father and I listened from the dining room. She told Mr. Skupa what I'd reported him doing. Then silence. Somewhere along the hallway, before she swung back through the connecting door, her face had softened. Rudy had apologized. He had assured her his reckless act wouldn't happen again. My father studied his poached egg, the yolk leaking into his toast, now cold. Flushed, ashamed of himself, he burped. "McGavin's." Unavailable, Maria's homemade flax loaf while she was still abroad. He said nothing more, flexing his watchband as if late for the office. Mr. Skupa, his business friend, had accepted blame for what both of them knew was my lie about his own wanton lapse. I had rescued my father by slandering Rudy. It was a debt my father now owed to each of us. And one, in turn, I owed to Rudy for not telling my mother the truth.

There seemed no reason for him to have admitted guilt, except that I was dear to him. Dearer, it felt, than I was to my father. At that age I was too young to consider the possibility that someone might be currying credit with someone else to do with the wholesaling costs of air conditioners. Or even that I myself might be currying favour with one parent over another, by covering up for him, even at the risk of losing Rudy's on-going approval.

Flamboyant and receptive, not a dry stick like Maria, he had permitted me to smooch him good night. "And I thought you were shy, Denise! You were ready to chop off the King's head!" Theatrically, extending his hand: "Give me your money or your life!"

My mother had been happy to accept his apology because it was easier to overlook *his* offense than it would have been my father's. Rudy was fun, his crime and the evidence in my bedroom soon forgotten. My father, following his travelling salesman's courtship of her in the thirties, mainly by fountain pen, had married his go-getter girl in Kelowna, where she was a waitress at the Royal Anne. *Dearest Cynthia* . . . I have his letters written in a compact hand talking up coastal life and breaker switches. My mother avowed more than once that he'd married her at the behest of his own mother to escape the war draft; his father's business needed him more than his country did. He brought her back here to a better life: car, clothes, eventually me, my younger brother: and he learned to tolerate her evolving cultural interests in exchange for her household flair and a willingness to go along with habits of his she found increasingly odious.

Such as pack-a-day smoking, snacking on Mars bars, and the way he failed to discipline his daughter except with the softest belt-strappings he could get away with in his study. Urging me to yelp loud enough for her to hear me downstairs in the kitchen. "Try a bit harder," he whispered. I would be draped over his knee like a fox fleece. Nothing he did hurt me, but neither did it not hurt me, his indifference to what a mother might be disciplining her daughter for. Mainly, in my case, some challenge to her notion of a mother's authority, though never for an offence deserving corporal punishment. He knew this, but that wasn't his fight. He also knew she wanted to get back at his irksome inability to discipline *himself*, and her thinking she could succeed by forcing his will on me.

She nagged till he took his puffing to the garage, and himself to disappearing, twice instead of once a week to his golf club. Where we suspected he lapsed regularly into syrup and French toast, only to endure her odd pleasure in scolding him for new levels of blood sugar that would kill him if the nicotine didn't. She abhorred any secret indulgence, especially in him. *Bacon too?* When home kits became available, she found she could revenge herself by forcing him to roll up his sleeve and jabbing an insulin needle into an unmarked vein, a gratifying act of selflessness on her part, while scolding his existence for its remarkable indifference, chiefly to her. He would buy her costly gifts, bracelet or stole, scarf or perfume, but she wouldn't be bribed into collusion if it meant excusing his "habits." She found fault with every gift, refusing to wear any of them when he was around, even sometimes when he wasn't, and returned to shops the ones she didn't mind the most.

*

When fighter jets in formation explode like a bomb overhead, I pause in my tidal trench for a moment's silence. It's anything but silent in their ongoing wake. I try not to tear up. Trailing smoke, above the city in a heartbeat, they're already streaking inland, headed for smaller and smaller cities in the direction of Hope. Of all towns over which to remind us of the dead—a million citizens and I sharing this pathetic moment as planes arrive *there* ahead of their sound.

> *It might be wise*
> *To weaponize*

For those fallen in battle, this moving but dismal tribute. Downtown in Victory Square, wreaths and the last post to ennoble a vague quest called freedom. A century of believing our dead fought to save the rest of us from enslavement and not themselves from dying. From realizing too late the Great Game was rigged against them despite their sacrifice in heading overseas. And now my mushiness in thinking everything they'd held dear might *not* have been vivid enough for them to blot out the madness and treachery had they lived.

That they were as vulnerable as the rest of us to memories so bland as to make dying not matter much to anyone, including themselves. Pondering their own despair as they perished.

I might bring this up over dinner. Surely Rudy's death had to be different. His sacrifice for Greta?

"Whatever," Patrick will say. "Still, I don't think you can reject emancipation as an abstraction. We actually fought for freedom."

"From what? The fairytale we went back to believing in, like hate won't repeat itself?"

"The Nazis."

"I've heard of them."

"I remember," he is going to repeat, "how shocked I felt hearing bacteria, not stress, might cause ulcers and be cured with antibiotics." It has become his favourite teaching moment. "Wasn't it the same with fascism? So-called incurable? We had to fight it with more than a lifestyle change. That's your abstraction, Denise. Lifestyle change."

He's more than the sum of his case studies, Patrick. That's why I admire him. Ulcers and fascism. Medication—*not* cruise-ship therapy. I'm uncertain how much he really believes in the lifestyle change endorsed in rehab clinics like Margaret's. Or in the one he'd like to endorse, minus current ethical guidelines, in his own clinic where he sets such a poor nutritional example. "Lifestyle change?" He's no more enamoured of this slogan than of the other called affirmative action. "Stress isn't the worst thing," he claims. He himself will never retire if it's just to relax. "You need to give your life to something, not change it."

"Like Rudy gave his?"

"Well, that might be pushing it."

"Maimed, mangled by inhuman men? And Margaret grieving, the affliction that's killing her?"

"She'll get over it."

"I don't think she's going to."

He thinks for a moment. "I might have to agree with you. Why?"

I like the way Patrick looks at me lately. I can still surprise him.

"Well, once Greta realizes she won't get over her loss, isn't that the first of her so-called twelve steps to recovery?" (There won't be time to come up with a better response than this one when I'm baking his *pesto crostini*.) "Accepting that she has something to live for, by tending his memory for reasons other than guilt?"

"Such as?"

"Gratitude? For taking her mind off food?"

"Really?" Not likely to be persuaded long by this one, once he starts eating. Especially the dessert I bought him at Meinhardt's.

"Denise, she helped him serve *meals* at the Living Room."

"To folks other than herself, yes."

"Not following you, sweetheart. Are you saying she should be grateful for her emaciated body?"

Well, this isn't quite the scenario I had in mind. Slow it down, let him have the last word—why not?—but remind him of his collusion.

"Gratitude to something more than *you*, Patrick."

"To me! I'm fat, I admit, but—"

"No, no. To something more than becoming a physician. *Your* hope for her."

"She preferred the alternative? Alliance with a skinny, mad, ex-air-con salesman?"

I suggest Rudy offered her an example . . . beyond eating, consumption, the gold-star career. "You know, beyond becoming her own heroine? Has your case history taken that into account?"

Yes, I like the way Patrick looks at me lately. I can still surprise him.

He pulls up a chair. "A mind of her own, our Margaret. Like quitting school on a whim."

His real fear is she quit medicine because he expected her to take up co-ownership of his clinic some day. This would be stubborn on her part. He feels her addiction to weight loss and the dope to assist it has been a ruinous extension of such stubbornness. Contrariness pivoting on perversity. Poor Rudy probably didn't stand a chance he thinks. When we thought he was manipulating her, she was actually urging him on. Persuading him to accompany her to Africa.

"We were hard on Rudy," says Patrick.

I'd lost touch with Rudy after that summer weekend when he installed the fridge and generator at our cottage. The truth is he'd endured my slander once, and had done so again. Not only had he forgiven me my childhood mendacity, assuming he remembered it, but also, these decades later, my unkind lament reported to him by Greta upon their arrival in Africa. That I—well, Patrick too— was full of anguish about his impact as an aging stick on our daughter's future. About her administering him palliative care and brushing his thinning gums. Probably also that we'd enjoyed ourselves, royally, at his expense, mocking his age and querying his motives while traducing their unlikely union—although never in her presence had we ever mentioned a goat or a raft.

Protesting, herring gulls ahead of me flap off the dry sand to catch the breeze. I wonder if I'll make it to the westernmost tide marker before the tide turns to stop me from reaching its ebb. There the shelf drops like a cliff into the sea.

"Freedom," I'll decide instead to respond, "from the lies we went back to believing in, like the free market?"

"Poverty," he is going to say.

*

The breeze freshens, bringing a scent of the timbered trusses ahead, clotted with mussels. The simple truth is, Rudy had given up smoking long before I'd asked him to babysit our Margaret. But after he began dating her, convinced of his self-gratification, I chose to remember ash on her bedspread. I failed to see that what I was looking at was the illusion that satisfied my assumption. He was old enough to be her grandfather.

His chronic carelessness was not something my mother could brush off, not the second time it happened. She never forgave him. Less so my father, who hoped for someone to talk to at the gala reception to which he had invited Rudy without getting my mother's approval. He knew she'd say no. Daddy never forgot a debt, no matter how small.

His debt also to me.

He paid for my trip abroad. This was after he arranged and paid for my termination, then illegal, at home. Today he might have suggested *going* to India for an abortion, not to forget one. It was the farthest away he could imagine, where what I needed to forget would be overwhelmed and even smothered by what a wholesaler friend had told him was the insistence there of gaudiness, confusion, poverty. My mother believed I was headed for Montreal, to "a home for unwed mothers," where I would give "it" up for adoption. Language of the era preceding the expected exile. Into which girls "in trouble" had been cast since we first welcomed the CPR with bunting—their mothers accompanying them to the station on Cordova. My mother railed against "the boyfriend," wouldn't speak to him when he called, hung up when he inquired after me. She certainly would not have connived at any plan to "get rid of it."

I wasn't sure I hadn't fainted. The painful wetness of my procedure in a tall office building off Hastings Street. Similar perhaps to what mothers like Judy say about forgetting the pain of childbirth.

My trip following did not free me so much as amend my horizon. Shortened it up inside colonial train stations, acquainting me with mobs instead of queues. I travelled with Norrie, daughter of my father's wholesaler friend, whom he'd met in Montreal at a trade fair. She had never been to India either, and visiting her extended family in Bangalore seemed a ripe idea for what I was now calling my "gap" year. My mother took this to mean a year dedicated to "amnesia" as I awaited the birth of my child in Quebec. It was neither a year, nor was it forgetful, except in the sense she hoped it would be, in putting my shame behind me.

"Leaving it all behind," agreed my father, "will be beneficial."

The spring weekend I came home, she dragged him and me to see Joan Sutherland in a production of *La Traviata*. My mother, a member of the opera association, was hosting afterwards the cast reception and having it catered. She insisted the three of us dine first at an old frame house on Seymour, Iaci's, but when we climbed the front steps she was surprised by the dining room and said for a recommended restaurant it felt like a bed and breakfast. Seven diners constituted a full house. Her Royal Anne might have served a mediocre table d'hôte but at least it had had booth-space for elbows.

Looking over the menu she said, "It's a miracle she and her husband keep coming back to this city. They've put us on the opera map. In exchange for what? Spaghetti and meatballs?"

My father turned to me without conviction. "Cynthia tells me there's a song in it I'll like, sung by a father." His finger traced the limited offering of dishes on the daily sheet. "What's focaccia?" Roast beef was his preference. "I hear she's a very large woman."

His amusement, expressed at either side of his mouth, was described by Patrick as the sound of air hissing intermittently from a tire. A kind of leaky chuckle, more bladder blockage than heartfelt discharge. Young Dr. Fitzgerald had then gone on, unkindly I thought, to yoke the prostate gland to an inner tube. It made me laugh.

"It's her *voice* that's divine," said my mother, "not her figure. I imagine Mr. Bonynge has been encouraging her to slim down."

"It ain't over till the fat lady sings," he rejoined, hissing happily. "Can't say I'm *not* looking forward to that." He put up with these occasions as part of their marital contract.

"Keep your voice down, Larry." My mother glanced at the bay-window table, inches distant, and then for some reason the floor, probably cat hair.

"Speaking of Mr. Bonynge's good work," said my father. "You're probably watching your own figure, Denise." An odd thing to say to me, unless he was colluding in the sham of my full-term pregnancy. India, after all, wasn't where I'd gone to put on weight. My mother preferred to ignore my figure and the supposed adoption of her grandchild by francophone strangers. His remark resembled what fathers might have presumed to advise daughters about catching a man after girdles had relaxed their grip on fashion. I'd never needed one, although for a while had tugged one on against Barry, which hadn't worked. My mother still wore one.

"I would suggest the aubergine to start," she said.

The wine arrived. Something called calamari my father nibbled at. When he got grumpy over his Veal Scallopini with Brown Butter and Capers my mother said what did he expect when he smoked so much, he had exfoliated his taste buds.

She was annoyed he'd ignored her suggestion that a diabetic should order the Pasta Primavera with Roasted Vegetables. When his meal had come, he embarrassed her by calling back our waiter with a request. Winking at me, he then shook his wrist uncontrollably, like a spastic person, something he couldn't do over my mother's meals without consequence. Seasoning her dishes not only insulted the chef but constituted grounds for extended banishment to our garage under the coach house.

After dessert, a panna cotta whose sweetness he relished deeply in front of her, he put down his napkin and reached casually into his tuxedo to remove a narrow velvet box. Black. He said nothing of course about celebrating my return from abroad. Instead, he said he understood there was to be a ballroom scene in the musical we were going to see, and that I'd probably need to wear something special to feel in tune with the music. He had clearly upstaged my mother, who looked astonished at his presumption.

"You'll probably want to return whatever it is," she said, pivoting to me.

When I opened the box, he reached over to help me lift from it a long strand of pearls, which he stood to clasp carefully around my neck. My mother, her eyebrows still raised, was fingering her own strand. She must have bought that one for herself. He then sat down and lit a cigarette, pleasing himself by blowing a perfect smoke ring on his first blow—pleased too, perhaps, for having forgiven me my moral lapse, without ever mentioning my moral lapse, which my mother had remained on the fence about without appearing to have lost her poise. She stirred her coffee. Studying me. She resented my evolving independence, the kind of worldliness I now wore, and not just around my neck, since returning from exile.

"When you have a family," my father loudly suggested, "you can pass the pearls on to your favourite." He actually said this, knowing what I knew and he now very much regretted. The bay window turned, the couple at it intent this time to appraise the princess rather than her pearls. I could only suppose he was thanking me—partly for lying about his lapse years ago, on my bedspread—mainly these days for betraying nothing to my mother of his arrangement of and payment for my abortion. He had gently told Jack, my soon-to-be-ex-boyfriend, that all would be well if he didn't interfere by offering, for example, to marry me. He called him Jack. Barry went on to become for a while the concertmaster in Calgary. Ironically, my mother would have approved.

I suppose, looking back, my father enjoyed this doubling down on her. It was the moral equivalent for him of balancing his jolly numbers on invoice sheets. He was colluding to deceive her about more than the abortion. It was strange, his compounding of duplicity in this way, making me a myth of sorts in the eyes of a daughter I would never have.

I did wonder, if Mother were to pass her own pearls on to me, whether I'd be keeping both strands lustrous by some acquired faith in family heirlooms and a mild Swedish soap. I was their only child, after my younger brother died in our cottage at the age of eight. Much later, when I discovered my strand of pearls missing after Greta hoisted it to buy herself another celebration of light—or whatever she experienced shooting up—I wondered. Did she think I wouldn't miss mine, if she left behind my mother's strand to deceive me in its own velvet box?

When in time I didn't seem to be having any more children, my mother put this down to my hooking up with Patrick rather late in life. Also, she believed I liked my own company a smidge too much. My father knew the truth, knowing my trip abroad had not extinguished the real reason for my going—to forget what had gone wrong back here. I was still grieving the loss of what I'd expected my life to become. It was like the opera that evening. I felt Violetta's heartache keenly. But at least I wasn't dying as she was of consumption. I remember her gay aria at the masked ball—and at my mother's reception following, at our house, the cast's glittering recitative continuing to sound quite hopeful for her recovery.

*

Over dinner I do plan on talking to Patrick. Not about the Nazis and such, but rather his day. Watching his patients come and go, talking of . . . Viareggio. A patient with liver disease and a rare attitude is planning to call in at this Italian port by cruise ship. "Giving her life over to rest," he tells me, "before the last port." He has suggested sailing with her sister.

"Terminal is it?"

He brightens. "At least Margaret has a future. She's got Medicine to come back to."

This remains his scenario: Margaret Fitzgerald, M.D.

Mine on the other hand goes:

"Do you still have your *agent* patient?"

"Who?"

"The real estate agent?"

"I don't think she's been in for a while. We don't do botox. I sent her to the dentist."

"Patrick, I'm thinking of selling the house. We're getting a bit creaky to give banquets anymore. I am, anyway. The place needs a steward if not a vassal."

And he'll be shocked, of course, when I also tell him where Greta now is.

Judy visited me a month less a day after Patrick and I took her by ferry to the rehab clinic. I brewed her a cup of matcha in the kitchen. Said Judy, "You aren't the wicked stepmother after all, Denise." With Judy you never quite knew what she intended by such a remark, but she seemed to sense my disappointment at not being able to talk to Margie the way she could. I think she was trying to alleviate my shame at having compelled Greta to share my unkind remarks about Rudy, with Rudy, in Africa. These apparently then leading to his self-exile. Judy herself remained as alleviated as ever from shame—at least in regard to abandoning her infant daughter—and had recently visited Margie at Margie's request.

She was instructed not to tell Patrick. She was to talk only to *me*, whom Margie feared she'd offended by not sharing her plight when I was eager to listen sympathetically. My offer to help had met with her frosty indifference. And so here I was, this time prepared to listen to the mother who wasn't really her mother, talking to the stepmother who actually was her mother, conveying a message from the daughter who no longer answered to either of us, but hoped for my forgiveness.

Judy was "permitted" to tell me Margie had checked herself out early from The Orchard, where we'd committed her. "She knows Patrick won't approve." She intended on her own to finish getting "better"—felt, in fact, she already was—in Whistler.

"Whistler," I said.

"Yes. And slowly putting on weight. She needs help to pay for a trailer she's sharing in Squamish with a girl from Melbourne. They were both hired at Araxia. Until her high-end tips start coming in, she needs a loan to stay afloat between meals. Serving them."

She described the trailer. "A leaky scow. I offered to buy her an outfit."

What impressed Judy was unexpected.

She had applied for her job as Margaret *Catalpa*. This at first puzzled Judy—the name change, but also why she bothered to mention it to Judy— unless, Judy decided— after her hoping some vague recognition of the name would impress a three-star employer—Greta also hoped to impress *me*. *My* name was Catalpa. "Unless, that is—I imagine it's possible—you once impressed *her*? Did you?"

Never nothing but direct, Judy could also be funny.

"I have no idea," I said.

"I suppose we were all young and gullible once, even Margie. *Here*," she said, handing me an envelope as if glad to be rid of it. "She asked me to give you this. I watched her scribble something down and lick it."

I tried to remember how I might have impressed Greta, enough to tempt her into abandoning Patrick's name in obeisance to the power or even terror invested in me as a stepmother. Judy was probably right, she needed money to survive until her tips accumulated and impressing me was worth disappointing her father. But it was strange. Greta knew I would have given her money, unconditionally. Just as I'd always kept her from going hungry.

"And then some," responded Judy. "It must have been for some other reason."

It stumped her. "*I* kept Patrick's name, I really don't know why she'd reject Patrick. I could understand not wanting to remind herself of me. But her father? Dr. Fitzgerald?"

I felt sorry for Judy. Even if she had never pined to become "Senora" Gonzalez, not even with the athletic señor's prize money pouring in, she could never be wholly persuaded that a motive for someone else's connivance in re-identifying herself would not involve the possibility of a windfall.

"Of course," I told Judy. "I can help her out."

"You can?" She sounded disappointed.

"Her father might resist. If it isn't for school."

"You know," said Judy. "This health thing isn't over. She told me she'd been suffering from Rickettsia, the aftermath of an old tick bite. I don't think it was ever drugs." Judy, rising to deposit her teacup in my dishwasher, studied my response to this bit of casual information. She was determined to trump whatever confidential scribble Greta's envelope contained. "Still," she said, "I think she took a risk checking out so soon."

Blue mountains over the bay. Breeze-scalloped seawater. And straight out at anchor a gleaming red-hulled freighter. An eagle touching down—but it doesn't—because ahead on the sand a hollowed-out flounder isn't worth its grabbing.

*

"Can we have a dog?" asked Greta.

It wasn't hard to persuade Patrick and his daughter to move out of their Kits townhouse after my mother had bequeathed her house to me. Welcoming Margaret I wanted her to know it wasn't always honeysuckle and croquet. How at her age I'd hated the reek of pulp rising overnight through the trees, after a mill miles up the sound released its toxic waste, counting on the stench to evaporate before city sleepers awoke. It could hang around for days if a heavy fog smelling of formaldehyde marinated its particulate matter of bleach and sulphur. A moaning foghorn, across the—

"Couldn't you just jump in our swimming pool?" asked Greta, her eyes wide.

"Not in wintertime."

I remember Japanese gardeners in white masks arriving in the fog with shears to prune the cherry, birch, witch hazel. Down the garden they—

"Couldn't you move?"

I once thought I had changed my life. I had in a way. Like Greta, when I returned from abroad, I didn't return to university. Unlike her I found the choices of my generation limited to nurse and teacher. A third was wife. No, librarian, then wife. Not until flying home did I think of stewardess, I liked the pipe smoke. A poem I remembered Barry showing me in the class we shared struck me as a warning, that when I got to be old, unless I could burn like fire and without smoke, there wasn't a lot of hope in any of these choices. He was hoping I would choose an abortion, a choice that wouldn't cloud either of our futures.

I attended Pitman Business College on Broadway and took speedwriting. It was easier than shorthand. I ate my lunch at The Aristocratic. These days you can't lunch without seeing a young person hunched over a communication platform, divining her device, if only to keep in touch with her date across the table. I sometimes think how far Barry and I might have got, keeping digitally in touch across the Pacific. A portable Olivetti might have helped me touch-type an aerogram; there was electricity at night to keep a diary. I suppose secretarial work amounted to the fifth option for young women, but it was really the first. Throw in double-entry bookkeeping, and when the chance came to move up from taking a boss' dictation, you could escape his Selectric—its spinning golf ball and attendant whiteout, less a calling than a scuffle—and begin balancing his costs and write-offs in a small office of your own, where you'd be treated with the respect of a male colleague for whom one knocked before entering.

With another course or two, I upgraded from stenography.

This got me a job in a dermatologist's office, followed by other medical offices. Risk, working capital, net profit. Dentists were the worst. Minding their books but also, too often, filling in for temperamental temps. Their casual attire reflected a new, relaxed attitude to showing up for work as professionals; dress whites giving way to jeans and coloured slacks. Tennis pros, Judy recently remarked, grunting through their service, have evolved into red shoes and lingerie. I had nothing better to do, living at home, than to develop a modest talent for interior design, heritage roses, erecting rockeries. Making a living wasn't the same as making a life. Even after I ended up living with Patrick, and continued to fill in at his clinic, it didn't end my temping for the temps, though it did land me a family: affectionate, comfortably nuclear, hungry. So I took up cooking. And started bringing Greta for walks at low tide in her little gumboots with dolphin insignias. We climbed down through the forest.

When Patrick hired me to go over his clinic's books, he claimed to remember meeting me at my father's golf club when he himself was a junior. I must have been celebrating, fifteen years earlier, my twenty-fifth birthday at a Sunday buffet with my parents. Although he'd never played with him, he was in awe of Daddy, who, having shone as a junior back in niblick days, still managed more than once as a senior to shoot his age. It seems improbable Patrick will ever match that feat, even with a generously fluctuating handicap. He called round at our house for his books. He was now overweight and his wife had recently left him. Daddy remembered him a little pitifully as a social member, his evaluation of non-family members embedded in numbers, not gatherings—in golf cards and invoice sheets, income-tax refundable and contracts bid on. Whom he owed or had out-foxed, profited by or donated to.

Or, in Barry's case, by the fact that he'd proposed to me over blackjack at a sorority fundraiser. Barry's capacity for numbers was not necessarily negligible.

My mother's album differed from my father's ledger. "I want to remember this" she might say of a bridge night out—hoping to savour what she knew my father wouldn't in a week recall as any more than his duty to keep her happy. A cocktail napkin embossed with a card player's regret, *Bid Me Adieu.* "Not me!" she would've certainly called out to him across the table. "Two diamonds!" A menu; minutes from an Elizabeth Fry meeting; Jewish war-orphan cards; receipts from a Maynards auction; a TUTS program for *Oklahoma!* If a souvenir were to be had by my mother, in it went, historical and quotidian both. Memento mori of more material substance deserved a box each of their own. Joan's hanky, for example, a prop stained with drops of tomato sauce—*it* had helped her sing the afflicted Violetta role in a tubercular-tinged voice. (My mother had insisted on Rudy handing this immediately over when she learned what he'd been gifted in our kitchen.) Also, a charred set of binoculars, through which you could still see through one barrel, rescued from our cottage after it burned to the ground

Primary sources, if I sell the house, I'll no longer have room to store.

*

I don't reach the tide-marker or pick mussels here before the tide turns and with it, I sense, the slackness inside me. Yes, probably I could give my life without having to change it much at all. Could either fall in love with my age or yearn rearward,

like Judy, to the age of late ass. I head back across
the sand and up-hill at a buttock-embalming lick.
Why would any woman drink the Kool-Aid of
blind marital faith when the recipe for self-accep-
tance is simply a virtuous resolution?

By the time I reach home, endorphins in satisfying flow.

Gas burner ticks before bursting into peaky
blue flames.

For Norrie and me, Varanasi was a mistake. Its
squalor on our itinerary north one more circle of
hell. Overbearing filth, stifling air, bringing senses
alive only to suffocate them. Out of my backpack,
an erotic carving of Shiva, to hold its fragrant san-
dalwood under my nose.

Norrie slipped on someone's excrement as we
made our way down a cobblestone lane to view the
ghats. These the hopeful destination of dying Hindus, already booked into "death hotels," until the
day their ashes would be released into the Ganges.
Moksha, said our guide, plucking my sleeve. The
practice of escape from an endless cycle of rebirth
as cow, cockroach, latrine cleaner. To renounce
the material world and accept *karma* enriched, he
said, your chances of *moksha*. Could I guess how
many logs were needed to burn, below us now on
the cremation grounds, a human person to ash?

Forests no doubt plundered to meet this
requirement of dying well. Bonfires glowing day

and night, the smoke an enduring toxic smog. A festive scene, the riverbank strung with a million shrouded lights. Relatives launching candles after dark to carry dead souls downstream, out of suffering into enlightenment. Casts of the afflicted gesturing after them as if through a scrim.

We wondered if widows still threw themselves onto pyres of disintegrating husbands. "They'd have to be insane," said Norrie. "Drugged," said the guide. "No more hope for living." Outlawed, it still happened when a husband's family shamed her into its expectancy. "Very not cognizant." At the train station next morning, Norrie observed loudly how glad she was to be born in Canada, where her own parents had shed their Hindu views. Had they remained *here*, she didn't know if she'd have been born at all. Or if she had been, survived. I thought she meant as secular Norrie, not orthodox Norindha. I didn't have time to take her seriously. She was *shouting* over the infernal din. ". . . And at the *end* of life, lucky enough to be married off to a hubble-bubble, can you imagine popping yourself onto his pyre!"

A mob of mostly men was clutching and grabbing at our saris, no more prophylactic than our Levis the day before.

I turn down the flame and add two pods of black cardamom to my simmering lamb-shanks. The risk of my current life. That I won't remember to remove these before ladling Patrick's dinner onto the mashed potatoes he likes. Sufficient thyme and cumin already potted.

"Are you sure she's really working? In Whistler, there's more dope than Shanghai."

"That's not Judy's apprehension."

"I hate Skupa," said Patrick. "I hate his diabolical memory."

"My dear Patrick. Are you old enough to remember the golden oldie . . . the line that goes, 'Stupid Cupid, stop pickin' on me. . .'?"

As voices go, in the rate and range of its vibrato, mine resembles a motorboat's.

I can't do my homework and I can't think straight
I meet him every morning 'bout half past eight
"Denise. Get a grip."
You mixed me up for good from the very start . . .
"You through?"
I'm acting like a lovesick fool . . .
"Denise, please!"

Mine isn't the aria to deliver him the daughter he wants. He isn't convinced Skupa-Cupid had the same effect on Greta. Is still shaking his head when he settles into his *panforte fichi e noci* with cream.

*

After dinner I settle down to go over house books. How to market a plus-size home without fear of its demolition, followed by feng shui fabrication of a brand new castle. Is there a remedy for conserving the romance of my family's modest descent? For staging the place for an Open when it doesn't matter if you stage it at all, since no one wealthy enough wants to move in without killing the lights and flattening its archive?

Diagnosis is easy—a case study of old city courting younger structures, slimmer lots—yet time also requires the hands-off counsel of Hippocrates. *Do no harm.*

A ledger isn't the only house book. In a diary I notice my speedwriting contraction for "skinny-dip . . ." Hardly the language of "current-liabilities" when you're looking to list and not noodle about in the looming downfall. Numbers are needed from "taxes," "hydro," "gas" to supplement a realtor's square-footage, full baths, acreage. Plus "revenue" from "accounts receivable"—had we ever accepted renters, and maybe should have—to tempt the profit motive of a buyer otherwise bent on demolition. My invoices go way back to the upkeep of a putting green my father inoculated every spring with Round-up, now a labyrinth, which I hired a stonemason to help me lay through the weeds. Here's his invoice.

Patrick wonders why I want to sell out, when our daughter's future in Whistler is far from settled. He agrees the house is too much for us to keep up, but since he isn't planning to retire any time soon the thought of its loss has upset him. He sometimes swims a few lengths in the summer, or sweeps the tennis court of maple leaves come fall, before inviting one of the young doctors round to his "humble abode" for a set. My surprise announcement has perplexed him. He's conflicted. *We may not need six bedrooms, or is it eight, but empty space as a satisfying reflection of the universe is a mirror he's quite content to look into every morning while he shaves, and a place at night to look around for leftovers in his slippers.* He supposes my father had hoped to have more children, another son at least, to carry on his family business.

He ponders this. "Why didn't he anoint you?"

"I wasn't his favourite."

The diary has distracted me. Not least some marginalia entered later, I notice, in speedwriting: "Nostalgia as surrender? When the past has temporary hold of you & the present offers not enough resistance to make the future a hopeful alternative?" I'm afloat in the night sea off Savary, admiring unstable phosphorescent waves lapping the dark sand. My father has waded in up to his hips—I can tell he's smoking a cigar, its tip aglow and the scent drifting lazily to me on the offshore breeze. Turning, I see in the moonlight Rudy treading water farther out. A chorus of Hebrew slaves is singing "Va, Pensiero" in the lighted cottage where my mother is making mellow use of our new generator to spin her LP. By now she has put my brother to bed and is walking down to the beach . . .

But enough wallowing in lost Eden. Greta's future has a better past than my family's conflagration. I'm sitting in the solarium where she used to tug a blanket backwards against Sandy's clamped teeth. Sandy was a beagle with scratchy nails and a barking fear of an itinerant coyote. Greta at six had close to seventy pounds on Sandy, gaining weight on him by the week, not to say traction. At nine, when she discovered he had fifty times the smelling power she did, she soon informed me that dogs smell in stereo, are capable of coordinating two sets of information at once, each nostril an instrument in harmony with the other to register new memories.

"His nose is a vault," she remarked. So was her Mac, I thought, from which she had extracted canine facts in impressive excess of her school assignment on "Cats." She was surprised we didn't possess a safe, even one in the wall, or have a safety-deposit box like Sandy's: a dog possessed many such boxes. I was enriched by her widening world at nine and her capacity to draw from it instructive analogies. At fifteen—the assignment "Hunger"—instead of Google she decided to try me.

The topic would normally have taken her no more than a half-hour to knock off with a trot down the information highway. Except she happened to recall I'd once been to India.

"You never know," Patrick whispered to me across the table. "Sometimes adolescence just wants to cuddle up."

I knew it was because the Wi-Fi was down.

It was an odd topic to assign an obese teenager, unless an ulterior lesson on the broader one of conspicuous consumption was intended. A day's fast might have proved a better lesson than a research essay. "Really?" cracked Patrick. I said nothing as she snacked on an after-supper pepperoni stick dipped in Dijon. Maybe I'd missed my calling to the classroom.

Pencil poised, she waited to scribble down my memories of third-world tribulation. Her already indecipherable scrawl, Patrick felt, was a sign from the Greeks she was destined to write prescriptions.

I recalled for her young men's waists in Bangalore, how you could wrap a man's tie around any one of them, twice. Arms on girls the circumference of liquorice whips. "Mom, that's racist." I explained I was exaggerating to make the case for hunger's scourge. She smiled and put down her pencil. She appreciated my help but it didn't appear useful, such hyperbole, in the case against hunger. I supposed she needed regions and statistics.

She asked why I'd gone to India. I mentioned Norrie. Our junket, together. Even what Norrie had casually said at the train station about not being born, had her parents stayed in India, or if they had, about not surviving. Greta wondered if she meant not having enough to eat. I said I hadn't thought of that, but no, it was something else.

"What, then?"

I think this was the first time after childhood Greta ever looked at me without seeming to know what I was about to say.

"Female infanticide."

She was surprised but not shocked.

"Killing girl babies?"

"Or fetuses."

"How come?"

"Maybe your teacher should assign the topic."

He didn't have to. She was soon pestering her class to raise money for . . . but the cause lacked sufficient definition—or so this "geog" teacher decided—to persuade potential donors it was possible to find a suitable destination for funds she might hustle before the end of school term.

"He mainly thought it was *extra-jurisdictional*." She imitated his tone while wobbling her jowls. Palms on her bountiful adolescent chest. "I don't see what the end of term's got to do with it."

She spread her notes. I later found them stashed upstairs in a drawer full of old candy wrappers.

"Don't worry," I told her. "You and I can start a foundation some day."

I mused wryly about growing our house's population with unmarriageable daughters, including me. "You?" It was no more than a high-minded statement you share with a teen whose ascendant standards are in need of ongoing support to keep them from receding too soon. With Greta, now swimming every week—often against the current and getting high on exercise—nothing worried us less than the tide going out on her standards, unless concerning her diet, for which her standards as well as ours remained irredeemably slack.

"You?"

"Well, sort of me," I responded.

And decided to share my reason for going to India. Unfortunately, it didn't make as deep an impression as I hoped. Confessions can be self-satisfying and she may have sensed preening. I shared with her the tale of my termination and my non-marriage to Barry. I didn't mention my non-marriage to her father. Oh, and yes, how I couldn't have any more children. I could have been wrong; I mean about her response. She sat patiently, not knowing what to do with her pen. I had embarrassed her, or else she felt I'd embarrassed myself. The thought of a sibling, even a half-sibling, no longer viable might have touched her, but it didn't cause her any noticeable grief.

I went on to recite from memory the poem Barry had shared with me in our class anthology, the day we discussed my abortion, calling it my "old-girl's" motto. More hyperbole, I feared. *Without smoke / that is how / good old wood / burns / that is how / I want to live / to give / fire without / smoke to be / fire.* "Miriam Somebody," I told her. "Her words stuck. I don't really know what they've got to do with hunger."

When I opened Judy's envelope, I saw with surprise what Greta had scribbled down. These same lines, guessing instinctively where they ought to break, in the idiosyncratic way I suppose she remembered me carefully reciting them. I took a while to translate why I felt so moved, but also why she'd bothered. Maybe to remind me in her barely discernible hand of my youthful resolution? If she was willing to take my name—hey Mom, was I living up to mine? She must have wondered, when I was making fun of her and Rudy, whether my old motto hadn't since gone up in smoke. And her memory of my cynicism, a smouldering reason for having refused to talk to me about her bodily attrition.

Who am I kidding? She needs a loan!

Leaning on her creditors, playing upstage to their conceit. As Judy believes, softening me up.

Still, the scenario I prefer is the one I intend putting to her father at breakfast tomorrow.

"A proposition, for her future?"

"Let's hear it."

I tell him. My scenario, unlike his, has her in the leading role of travelling director for a family foundation devoted to the elimination of female infanticide. A private operation like my father's. Accountable, of course, but this time of profit to more than just one family.

"I don't believe it."

Believe it I tell him. She just needs to let us know she's onboard. Come to see us, agree she might like to afford her life another option. In return, we would agree Patrick's clinic no longer seems, if it ever was, her first choice.

"I beg to differ."

I show him Greta's schoolgirl notes on hunger, in the indecipherable hand he favours as a physician. He's tickled he can't read them. *Gls r_ lk b po Hnd p_s cs c- a d_re ss . . .* Speedwriting was a skill that impressed her and which she quickly picked up from me. As I do with his clinic's books, I summarize for him what here amounts to the mission statement she and I would soon formulate: *Girls aren't welcome by poor Hindu parents because of a dowry system, and then, if they manage to barter a marriage through debt, a daughter isn't just lost to a husband's family but enslaved by them as the extra cost of housing her.*

I've doctored up her transcription. Slovenly punctuation, ditto syntax. The main goal of the Catalpa Foundation will be to help Indian NGOs educate Hindu families inclined to eliminate the costly birth of girls by eradicating them.

"You're dreaming," says Patrick. "The cost of dowries will just skyrocket. Why don't you think instead of subsidizing *polyandry*?"

"Or jobs?"

I confess part of all this is to give my life over to making it smaller.

"Downsizing," he says, "isn't exactly *giving* your life. It's just changing it.

He misses his daughter. Who, he wonders, erased the sea from her heart?

*

I wander upstairs after dinner to survey the cost of the future. I've sorted through taxes, utility bills, plumber invoices, records of gardeners' wages and roofing costs, statements from the Land Title and Survey Authority, the deed my father once procured from the retired shipping mariner who built our house before the war. The First One. None of this file will discourage a wealthy new owner from building an even larger house looking farther out to sea.

Knock knock?

I enter the bedroom once mine, then Greta's, before she shut me out. I intend to make the house difficult to destroy without also razing this same room we both dreamed in. I hope to commission an artist to paint its walls. An esteemed artist, who will agree to support our commendable cause against infanticide. How can she refuse? Public participation on her part would guarantee from the city the same heritage designation this artist herself enjoys. Am I dreaming?

Mother introduced us years ago at a church bazaar. She had bought one of her early canvases at a small gallery off Main called Grunt. It amused her to pronounce its name. (Surprising, as she'd long raised the drawbridge against "fart.") I remember we'd agreed to bake pies for the bazaar, before asking Maria to spend a day in our little orchard picking cherries to mix into crusts. Mother's philanthropic sense, like mine, was based on others pitching in.

Will it help?

Her reputation as a sculptor, painter, video artist has ascended to old-master status, so even if the house's preservation isn't assured, her walls will guarantee greater leverage for our foundation in the sale to establish it. She's given her life to burning brighter with age. The destruction of a late mural by her would amount to a national scandal. I'll suggest to her the whimsical theme of Princess

Mouseskin's bosky exile. Who knows but that Greta's posters from anatomy class, still pinned to the walls, won't inspire their replacement with dancers, servants, dogs. Invite her to go further! An installation! Stuffed tunics, ceramic slippers. Even a skin to step out of. A soundscape of dishes, goblets, royal remorse. A banquet for the ages.

Not beyond her, the rekindling of a father's love.

Rudy had arrived that evening, I remember, his breath smelling of cigarettes. He had something to share before tucking me to sleep. A gift for the little princess. First he lifted my window, sliding carefully closed on its rings the velvet curtain. A late robin nesting in the laurel, the tick of lawn sprinklers below. Twilight extinguished, my bed lamp coming up.

My bedspread pulled back to reveal a swelling between the sheets.

Then this illustrated *Grimm*, a book he extracted to let me touch it, calfskin covers tinged with the scent my mother abhorred.

He opened it and began to read, his voice in my ear pitched deeper than a mineshaft. Turning pages, by the end no longer reading them. He had the lines by heart. *I'd rather die than eat such food.* At the last line, pausing for breath, he inhaled the whole scene before blowing it skyward in a long dispelling stream. Not smoke, but the essential element of his voice alone. Delighted, I snuggled deeper into its scent and heard him whisper, as he prepared to leave me . . . *Now that he had found her again, she was more dear to him than his kingdom and all the jewels in the world.*

*

Judy was right, if for the wrong reason. But has taken no comfort in her suspicion of a relapse. Our daughter was found dead of a suspected fentanyl overdose in the driver's seat of the little car we bought her to visit us in, now and then, downtown.

We look west to the fireworks and the Salish Sea.

We were expecting her that week. At our smaller, repurposed table.

Her car was discovered over-parked on Powell Street, her bloated body slumped across the wheel. At first she had looked like a young man. From her coat pocket, the police retrieved an oblong box containing my pearls. I had continued to think, as she settled into her serving role in Whistler, that she had been looking forward to her life on behalf of the dowry-less in the real, afflicted world. Now, I wasn't sure. It would have made all the difference to us both.

Keath Fraser won the Chapters / Books in Canada First Novel Award for his 1995 novel *Popular Anatomy*. His stories and novellas have been published in many anthologies in Canada and abroad. Collections of his short fiction include *Taking Cover* and *Telling My Love Lies*. The volume *Foreign Affairs* was short-listed for a Governor General's Award and won the Ethel Wilson Fiction Prize. He is the author of *As For Me and My Body*, a memoir of his friend Sinclair Ross; and of *The Voice Gallery*, a narrative of his far-flung travels among broken voices. The royalties from his international best-selling anthologies *Bad Trips* and *Worst Journeys: The Picador Book of Travel* were given to Canada India Village Aid (CIVA), the late NGO founded by George Woodcock. A selected stories, *Damages*, is forthcoming from Biblioasis in May 2021.